THOSE WHO LOVE

THOSE WHO LOVE

Denise Robins

Chivers Press • Thorndike Press
Bath, England Waterville, Maine USA

This Large Print edition is published by Chivers Press, England, and by Thorndike Press, USA.

Published in 2002 in the U.K. by arrangement with the author's estate.

Published in 2002 in the U.S. by arrangement with Claire Lorrimer.

U.K. Hardcover ISBN 0–7540–4889–6 (Chivers Large Print)
U.K. Softcover ISBN 0–7540–4890–X (Camden Large Print)
U.S. Softcover ISBN 0–7862–4237–X (General Series Edition)

The text of this Large Print edition is unabridged.
Other aspects of the book may vary from the original edition.

Set in 16 pt. New Times Roman.

Printed in Great Britain on acid-free paper.

British Library Cataloguing in Publication Data available

Library of Congress Cataloging-in-Publication Data

Robins, Denise, 1897–
    Those who love / Denise Robins.
        p.   cm.
    ISBN 0–7862–4237–X (lg. print : sc : alk. paper)
    1. Large type books. I. Title.
    PR6035.O554 T48 2002
    823'.912—dc21   2002022309

ƒ

CHAPTER ONE

It was with very mixed feelings that Peta Marley boarded the liner at Bombay that Saturday morning.

Her main sensations were of relief because the heat in the train these last few days and nights, travelling from Calcutta, had been terrific, and down on the quay, dotted with swarms of screaming natives, the temperature and the noise were unbearable. Certainly it was good to come on board an English ship and find sudden peace; cool, washed decks under the striped awnings, cool-looking, immaculate officers in their white uniforms, and a nice English stewardess waiting to see what she could do for you in your cabin. That was a relief, and so were the first few moments sitting on the edge of the bed mopping a streaming face, combing back damp curls, and realising that the other bed wasn't to be occupied.

Peta would have the cabin to herself—as far as Gib. anyhow. Thank heaven for that!

The suspicion of a breeze blew through the porthole and made Peta gasp and shut her eyes.

'That's good!'

'Is this your first voyage, miss?' asked the stewardess.

'No,' said Peta. 'I came out here a year ago to take a job in Calcutta, but like a fool I found the climate too much, and I've spent most of the time in and out of my bed.'

'You'll be all right now. The voyage'll pick you up,' said the stewardess, feeling sympathetic, because she thought that the young lady looked a little frail. The sun tan was deceptive. Such a pretty young thing, too, with her slim figure, her dark curls, and big expressive eyes with lashes such as the stewardess had only seen on film heroines.

When the stewardess left her alone, Peta forced her limbs into action and in an exhausted fashion began to unpack her suit-case. The first thing she drew from it was a small framed snapshot of an extremely good-looking man leaning against a palm, smoking. Then her expression changed and a more vital look came over her small face. Her eyes assumed a rapture which she expressed in a whispered breath:

'Auburn!'

But almost immediately the vitality departed. She became listless again, put the photograph down, and in a half-resentful fashion began to throw silk pyjamas, brush and comb, and sponge bag on to the bed.

Gone were all the feelings of relief that she was on board ship and about to go home.

She even felt a sensation of panic at the idea of leaving this India. For all its noise and heat and the climatic conditions which had defeated her, it was a place of glamour, of colour, and had been glorified for her because it was here she had met Auburn Lyell.

She had said good-bye to Auburn in Calcutta, and since then had known no real peace of mind. With painful vividness she recalled the hot, turbulent station and Auburn, who came to see her off, holding both her hands and telling her that they would soon meet again. She was leaving him behind, but he would be in England before she was, for he was flying over. He might even meet the liner at Tilbury, he had said. He wanted more than anything to see her again. When the train started and she was leaning out of the window, he seized both her hands and kissed them, ran along the platform with the train, still pressing his lips to her palms until he could do so no more.

'*Au revoir*, you sweet thing, and *bon voyage*!' he had called after her, waving his topee wildly.

She had huddled back in the corner of the train ashamed of her tears, ashamed of the intense feeling which he roused in her. She was in love with him. She had no right to be, she told herself, because he hadn't asked her to marry him. But he was going to ask her. She was pretty sure of that. He had suggested it on that night at the club when Mrs. Bradley, who was Peta's employer, had kindly allowed her to

3

accompany them to a dance, and they had left the small boy to whom Peta was nursery-governess in charge of an ayah.

At that dance, Auburn had taken Peta in his arms and sealed her lips with the kisses of a lover—the first Peta had known. He had told her that she was a little witch and that she had cast a spell over him and that there wasn't another girl in the world who had ever made such a complete slave of him.

He had made her admit that she was in love with him, too, and that she wanted to meet him again when they were all in England. And after that she hadn't seen much more of him. Her peace of mind had been shattered and she had fallen in love only to be confronted by a dozen minor misfortunes, all of which prevented her from meeting Auburn. First of all he had gone away on business, and going away in India meant days of travel. Then she, herself, had gone down with severe fever, and, while she was still recovering, Mr. Bradley had received an urgent cable which took him back to his business house in London. Mrs. Bradley and the boy went with him. They had not wished to leave the young governess behind, but she had a touch of dysentery, and the doctor had advised her not to travel till she was fitter.

Peta had had to do what she was told, but it was not much fun being left in a nursing-home in Calcutta, besides which she felt a failure,

4

although the Bradleys had been very kind and had told her that her job would still be open to her when she rejoined them in London. But it wasn't the thought of her job that worried her half so much as the thought of Auburn Lyell. Mrs. Bradley, who had known him for years, had warned Peta that 'Burn,' as he was nicknamed, made love charmingly to most pretty women and meant nothing by it.

Did he mean anything by his love-making to *her*? Yes, surely he did! When he came to see her off, he had repeated all the marvellous things he had said at the club when he had first made passionate love to her.

Peta, sitting alone in her cabin waiting for the ship to sail, alternated between hope and despair, and wondered if she had been absurd to frame the snap-shot which he had given her, or absurd to find herself remembering with such poignancy that tall, lithe figure, the gay brown face which looked even browner because of the bleached fairness of his hair and the brilliant blue of his eyes.

'Stop being a little fool, Peta Marley,' she admonished herself fiercely, 'and remember that Auburn Lyell has heaps of money, knows masses of pretty women and wouldn't be serious about an impecunious nursery-governess!'

She was not in the least cut out to be a nursery-governess, and she knew it. She was too spirited and fond of life, and it couldn't be said that a daily existence with a spoilt little boy, teaching, washing, ironing and sewing, was in the least enthralling. But she had no alternative. She was the daughter of a retired doctor, a widower, and had received just an ordinary good education and been trained for no career. When her father had died a year ago, leaving her practically penniless, she had entered a general hospital, taken some training, and been forced to retire because she was not strong enough to stand it. After which she took the first job that came her way, and considered herself very lucky to go abroad with the Bradleys as a nursery-governess to their son, Derek.

Someone parted the striped curtain which hung in the doorway, and came into the cabin. A Goanese steward with two suit-cases, followed by a slightly built man in grey flannels, unmistakably British.

Peta confusedly pushed behind her some lingerie which she had been unfolding and rose to her feet.

The steward said:

'Cabin No. 14. First Class—must be right. Not for lady. This is for gentleman.'

The Englishman said:

'I'm frightfully sorry, there must be some mistake.'

Peta said:

'I was shown in here. I'm sure this is my cabin. It was booked for me in advance by Mr.

6

Bradley, of Calcutta.'

The man in grey pulled out a sheaf of papers, dropped his passport, picked it up again, and searched for the necessary paper to prove that he had not made an error.

'Frightfully sorry,' he repeated. He had a charming voice and beautifully shaped hands, two things which Peta was quick to notice. She judged people on their voices and their hands. 'My name's Frensham. Dr. Frensham.'

Ah, thought Peta, the medical profession! Hence the nice hands. And it gave her a friendly feeling, dear old Daddy having been a doctor. She gave the intruder that swift, sudden smile which lit up her rather serious young face.

'Well, one of us must be wrong,' she said.

Noel Frensham examined his papers. He was in no mood to notice that the girl was young and pretty or had an intriguing smile. He was much too tired and hot, and feeling far from fit. He said abruptly:

'I booked at the last moment, and was told that I couldn't have a cabin to myself, but was to share one with a Mr. Peter Marley.'

Light dawned on Peta, and she suddenly bubbled with laughter.

'How absurd! My name *is* Peta Marley, but it's P-E-T-A. That's the mistake they've made.'

Noel Frensham returned the papers to his pocket and looked at the girl in an exasperated way.

7

'I see. So sorry for disturbing you. A silly mistake.'

The steward, quick to sense a man who would tip generously, dropped the suit-cases and said:

'If the sahib will wait here—he need not trouble. I go to the office to make other arrangements. Think I can find cabin for sahib alone.'

'Well, thank the Lord for that,' said Noel Frensham crossly.

The steward fled. Peta said:

'Isn't the heat ghastly . . .' Then, being an observant person, saw that the doctor's thin face wore a distinct pallor, and that as he stood there, he flinched as though in pain.

She added quickly:

'Are you feeling all right? Would you like to come in and sit down?'

He accepted the invitation because the narrow ship's passage with its glaring white walls was suddenly swimming round him. He sank on to the edge of one of the beds in Cabin No. 14, and wiped his face. Peta looked down at him anxiously, poured him out a glass of water and handed it to him.

'I expect it's tepid,' she said, 'but there's nothing else.'

He took the glass she handed him and thanked her. Now he became aware that this girl had a sweet manner and soft, kindly eyes. His crossness evaporated. He felt ill and worn.

'Silly of me,' he said, 'but I precious nearly fainted just then.'

Peta shook her head at him.

'Physician, heal thyself!'

He gave a wry smile.

'Not so easy. I don't know what's wrong. I've had a confounded pain for the last fortnight.'

'Haven't you seen anyone?'

'Not had time. Been on holiday, hunting elephants, right away from civilisation. Only just got back in time to pick up this boat. Thought it would be better to get back to London if I was going to be ill.'

'Oh, but I hope you're not,' said Peta. 'So rotten when one doesn't feel well. I've had a lot of fever myself since I've been in India, and it does take it out of one, doesn't it?'

He nodded, pulled a cigarette from a thin gold case and lit it. Peta noticed that he had a clever forehead, the dark hair springing back vitally from it; keen hazel eyes, and a touch of austerity about the firm mouth.

Here, she was sure, was no ordinary man. No common practitioner. She was certain he was a man with a reputation. Frensham. She could not recall having heard the name. But there were so many hundreds of specialists—brilliant at their jobs and not known to the general public. This man might be any age. His figure was youthful, and so were his eyes, but the clever face was slightly lined, and the dark hair just tinged with grey behind the temples.

9

Noel Frensham, lighting a cigarette, was thinking:

'I wish to God *I* thought I had a touch of fever and nothing else. But I believe I picked up some mysterious bug in that infernal safari. Confound all the elephants in India. I want to get on with my work when I get home.'

The Goanese came running back and announced that he had found a cabin alone for the doctor sahib. Noel Frensham rose and repeated his apologies to Peta for the interruption.

Then she was alone to continue her unpacking, to forget the sick doctor, to remember nobody but Auburn Lyell, and to ask herself feverishly whether he would keep his promise to see her in London, or whether by the time he got back he would have forgotten her name!

CHAPTER TWO

The next time Peta saw Noel Frensham was a couple of days before they reached Aden. It was a terrifically hot morning.

The sea was hard and blue like a glittering stone in the sunlight. Most of the passengers lay gasping under the awnings on deck. But Peta felt restless. A queer, unsatisfied feeling which had been hers since she left Bombay—

and Auburn.

Despite the intense heat, she wanted to take exercise. She was really feeling quite herself again. The two days at sea had done her good, given her back her appetite. In a white linen dress showing her sun-brown back, and with a wide-brimmed linen hat on her head, she walked along the deck and eventually found, in a deserted spot, the doctor who had claimed her cabin by mistake. He was lying in a deck-chair—like one dead. He had that grey, exhausted look which had worried her when she first met him, but when he saw her, he came to life, nodded, and gave a faint smile.

'Ah! It's you. Hullo! How goes it?'

'Hullo,' she said, a trifle shyly, and, with her hands stuck in the pockets of the linen dress, looked down at him. Two pairs of eyes regarded each other through sun-glasses. Noel Frensham said:

'You're too energetic to be true. I can't move. I can hardly breathe.'

'Aren't you feeling any better?'

'Not much.'

'Seen the ship's doctor?'

'Huh huh! I had a few words with my worthy colleague last night. He just thinks I'm run down and got a bit of fever.'

'That isn't what you think, is it?' said Peta with some insight.

'To be frank, no,' said Noel. 'Not that I have the least idea what is wrong, but I'm full up now with various dopes, and once we're through the Suez Canal I dare say I'll feel different. I'd like to see a grey sky and feel a few spots of rain on my face, wouldn't you?'

' "England, my England!" ' quoted Peta.

'One doesn't really appreciate all that the poets say until one has been abroad any length of time!'

'Perhaps not,' she said. 'But I loved being in India. I thought it was wonderful. The climate was too much for me, which was maddening. It *is* sickening to have a willing spirit and weak flesh.'

Noel Frensham took off his glasses and wiped them wearily.

He was feeling that way himself at the moment. And there was nothing he loathed more than sickness of body when his mind was abounding with vitality, with unlimited thirst for knowledge and the keen zest for life.

'Don't stand up,' he said suddenly to the girl beside him. 'Sit down and have a talk.'

She pulled a chair up near him, laced her arms behind her head, and drew a long breath. The ultramarine blue of the water looked a strange hot purple through her tinted glasses.

'Where do you practise?' she asked. 'I've a friendly feeling for the medical profession, because my father was a doctor.'

Noel Frensham tried to forget that he ached in every bone in his body and interested himself in the girl. She was rather a dear, he

12

thought. He liked her lack of affectation. So she was a doctor's daughter, was she? He encouraged her to talk about herself. Peta proceeded to tell him sufficient to acquaint him with the type of life she had been leading. Fairly dull. She had had an ordinary sort of upbringing, a lot of domestic responsibility after the death of her mother when she was only sixteen and a half, and enforced economy once her father, who had practised in the suburbs, had retired. Then, after his death, Peta's attempt to stand a hospital training, and subsequent failure. He was sure that she was not fitted to be a hospital nurse, this child with her slim, frail body and rather intense young face. Not the type. How old was she? Twenty-one or two. He grimaced. He was nearly double her age and felt it.

Noel Frensham was a psychologist, interested in the healing of mind as well as bodies. And before Peta Marley had talked much more about herself he realised that there was less for Peta to worry about, as far as her constitution was concerned, than there was in her mental attitude. She was the reverse of the typical modern girl with her premature knowledge about life and her contempt for Victorian sentimentality. Peta Marley was more Victorian than any young woman who had yet come his way. A soft, gentle thing with a romantic outlook. Not too good in these days, mused Noel Frensham, when it pays to be hard-boiled. And because she was gentle, she was sure to get more than her share of the knocks. Somehow he didn't like the idea of her having to work for her living and take any job that was offered. She spoke of the Bradleys. They were exceedingly nice to her and generous. But she dreaded the idea of looking after their spoiled son and heir for years! Noel sympathised. And what about her romantic side? He made Peta reveal more of herself. By a little manoeuvring he was able to discover that she had never been engaged nor had more than an innocuous boy-and-girl affair at home in the old days. But there was a man in whom she was interested. She was careful not to give away his name. She just said that she had 'met someone in Calcutta' who was 'simply marvellous,' and that she was hoping to meet him again in England.

Then she seemed to become aware that she had been drawn into talking too much about herself, and flushed and confused, apologised for it.

'But don't,' said Noel; 'I've enjoyed hearing it all.'

'Do you know,' she said, 'you haven't yet answered my first question to you.'

'About my practice? Oh, I've got a consulting room in Wimpole Street.'

She had felt sure that he was *someone*. He was a heart specialist, he told her.

'H'm,' said Peta. 'You know how to treat

14

angina and valvular diseases, and that sort of thing. But you haven't yet found a way of curing a broken heart, I suppose?'

'There isn't such a thing, and neither does the heart feel all these emotions attributed to it. They're in the brain,' he said dryly.

'Doctors are always so practical,' said Peta. 'You sounded just like my father then. I remember, when my mother was alive, he used to sit on us both, unless we were authentic to the letter. We weren't allowed to romance about anything. Do you treat your family in that harsh way?'

'I'm sure I should if I had one, but I haven't,' said Noel. 'I'm a lone bachelor!'

Peta eyed him thoughtfully. There was something very attractive about this man. She wondered why he should be nearly forty and still a bachelor. But his next words washed out any belief that he had had an unhappy affair in his youth. He said:

'Since I qualified I've been much too busy with my job to get a wife and face those sort of problems.'

That was true. He *had* been too busy. He was absorbed in his profession. Not that there weren't moments, during his vacations, for instance, when he grew suddenly lonely and felt the need of a soft feminine presence, and even children. He had made money. He was a rich man these days. But what was it all for? What was it leading to? He hadn't even a nephew whom he was fond enough of to make his heir.

That reminded him—he hadn't made a will. Foolish, perhaps, when there was that house in Wimpole Street, and the lodge in Scotland, a glorious place of quiet and rest way up in the Highlands, where he went to shoot and fish. It would be a pity to die intestate and let everything go to a distant cousin. He knew who it *would* go to. Young Kenneth Powell, whose mother had been a Frensham. Kenneth was at Oxford, had an effeminate face, long hair, and an aptitude for nothing much but playing the saxophone in a dance band. God, he'd hate all his possessions to pass into the hands of a young whipper-snapper like that.

But why turn his thoughts to dying just because he was feeling rotten and was depressed? He pulled himself together.

'I can see a steward approaching with a long iced drink for me. What about joining me, Miss Marley?'

'No, thanks awfully, and I'm sure you want to be quiet,' she added, getting up. 'I'll go on with my walk.'

He let her go. And after a few sips of the drink which the steward placed beside him, he shut his eyes and tried to forget the blinding pain across them. This wasn't fever. Neither was that other rotten pain anything to do with appendix, as that fool of a ship's doctor suggested. Any damn thing would be an appendix or a tonsil case for him. Noel wished he were home and could go up to the hospital to which he was honorary physician, and get an intelligent opinion.

His brain wandered on. Nice little thing, Peta Marley. What sort of fellow was she in love with? She didn't seem very happy about it with her mention of broken hearts. God, he felt hellish! A pretty thought if he passed out and was flung to the sharks in that nice bright blue water. He could see Kenneth Powell standing in his library getting hold of some bookseller from Charing Cross Road to come and clear out his beloved books—the collection of a lifetime. And the money. What would he do with it? Inaugurate a new jazz band.

At length the effects of drink and dope given him by the ship's doctor had their way with Frensham. He fell asleep.

That night he was missing from the dining saloon. Nobody noticed his absence except Peta, who had looked for him. Not for a long time had she found anyone that she enjoyed talking to more. There was a kind of quiet resolution, a dry wit about Dr. Frensham, which intrigued her. And he inspired confidence, made her talk about herself. She would like to tell him more about Auburn and her feelings for him, and see what Dr. Frensham thought about it.

Coming out from dinner, she met the Goanese steward who was in charge of Noel's cabin, and inquired after him. She was quite disturbed to hear that 'the doctor sahib' had retired to his bed because he felt worse. She decided to pay him a call and see if there was anything she could do. When she knocked outside his cabin door there was a growl of:

'What is it?'

'It's only Peta Marley,' she called back. 'I wondered if I could be of any service. I'm so sorry you're no better.'

The voice, less growling, said:

'Come in.'

She pushed aside the striped curtain and walked in. The cabin was scrupulously tidy, but the figure in the bed looked dishevelled, hot, uncomfortable. With his ruffled hair and a fever flush on his thin face, he seemed to Peta much younger. He gave her a half-hearted smile.

'Sweet of you to bother,' he said.

She drew nearer him.

'Don't forget I've had a year's training in a hospital,' she said proudly.

His smile broadened then.

'Well, Nurse Marley, and what's your valuable opinion?'

She blushed and laughed.

'I wouldn't like to give one. Nurses aren't supposed to, anyhow. But I do wish I could think of something to make you feel better.'

'I'm better for your visit,' he said gallantly.

It wasn't altogether untrue. Peta Marley

looked her best in evening dress, and pleased his vision. She had put on one of the prettiest frocks she possessed, pale-rose chiffon, with white flowers, which she had made herself. She was rather good at dress-making, and had worked hard to make herself a few nice clothes before she had accompanied the Bradleys to India. Auburn Lyell had liked this frock and had told her so in no uncertain language. It had a tiny cape to match, but it was too hot to wear that tonight. Slight though she was, she had a very beautiful throat and shoulders, white as milk. And under the chiffon, they were like 'rose-misted marble,' thought Noel, suddenly remembering a quotation from the poetry of his youth. She had exquisite hands, too, and the slenderest of ankles. An amazingly pretty child.

'You ought to be up dancing with all the young men,' he said.

'I'd rather talk to you.'

'That's flattering.'

'Not that you can want to talk if you feel ill.'

'I feel no better if I lie still by myself. The pain goes on.' She looked at his hollow eyes and that unnatural colour on his face and shook her head anxiously.

'Can't the ship's doctor do anything?'

'Nothing. But I dare say I'll be better in the morning. These attacks have been coming on and off since I left the jungle. They've been intermittent; I dare say I'll live through the night.'

19

He was joking, but she could sense that he was a little afraid behind the jest. Afraid because he didn't understand what was wrong, medical man though he was, himself.

There were mysterious diseases to be picked up in the East. Peta knew that. And she, too, was afraid for him.

She did not stay. She felt that he might drop off to sleep if she left him alone. But she begged that he would send for her if he needed attention during the night. She did know *something* about nursing.

'I'm sure you do,' he murmured, 'and thank you kindly. I won't forget. Now run upstairs and dance.'

But she did not dance. And she avoided the one or two young men who, attracted by her soft beauty, pursued her in the light manner of voyagers. Somehow the gay lilt of the dance band made her melancholic. The thought of Dr. Frensham, lying down there ill and in pain, was depressing. He was a stranger and meant nothing to her, but she *was* sorry for him. She went to a quiet part of the deck and looked up at the large brilliant stars which were shedding a metallic glow into the phosphorescent sea. She began to concentrate upon the memory of Auburn Lyell, the lithe, fair handsomeness of him and that way that he had of looking at you, talking to you, making your heart turn over. She could feel the burning imprint of his lips on her hand. Surely he wouldn't have done that if he hadn't meant it? Meant what? That he was in love with her? Why should she think that just because she had fallen so madly in love with him?

He was a very rich, important young man. His father was 'in leather,' and Auburn divided his time between the Lyell manufactories in London and Calcutta.

He had his choice of women. So many were crazy about him. Mary Bradley had told Peta that. But why believe what she was told? Much better to form her own conclusions. Auburn had been marvellous to her—paid just as much attention to the young nursery-governess as to any other women when there had been a party on at the Bradleys' bungalow in Calcutta.

There had been one particular evening when he had hinted that he was tired of sophisticated society women, of playing bridge with the Mrs. Brindleys of this world or exchanging smart repartee with the girls he met in town or out East. He found her, Peta, infinitely soothing, he had said, sweet and friendly. Not boring, as she had supposed. Well—why not believe him and believe that he would see her again—and again—when they got back?

She felt a sudden intense longing for him and to feel his kisses on her hands . . . on her lips, next time they met. She would like to be loved by Auburn as she loved him.

She went to sleep that night with her senses

held in a thrall by his memory.

CHAPTER THREE

They had reached Aden.

Soon after dawn Peta was up and on deck leaning over the rails marvelling, as she had marvelled on the outward journey, at that sinister rock rising out of the blue sea. Amazing red shore, red sky of the sunrise, and masses of little boats putting out to meet the boat like black dots, swarming over the glittering water.

Peta gave a short sigh. It seemed five years rather than five days since they had left Bombay. And now India was a long way off. They had been five queer days for Peta. She had not mixed much with the other passengers, gossiped or danced or played games, as she had done on the voyage over with the Bradleys.

She had devoted quite a lot of her time to Dr. Frensham, whom she was quite sure by now was a very sick man. True, the ship's doctor could find nothing much wrong with him, and Noel kept struggling up, then going back to bed. But Peta had watched him growing perceptibly thinner and weaker. She was quite worried. The more she talked to Noel Frensham, the more she liked him. She had told him quite a lot about The man, too, without mentioning any names. After all, it wasn't fair to give away Auburn's name, because, although he had made love to her, she had no right to broadcast the affair. But it was good to talk about it to someone, and Noel Frensham was so understanding. A bit of a cynic, perhaps. In his dry fashion he had warned her against believing all that was said to her on an Eastern night when men and women were apt to be swept away by the beauty and warmth and glamour.

And Peta had laughed and said: 'Oh, I know . . . I'm not counting on anything . . .' But that was rather more bravado than anything. She *was* counting on Auburn and what he had said, no matter how idiotic it seemed.

The deck was fast filling with passengers eager to look upon land after the five days at sea. Peta began to feel hungry and walked towards the dining saloon. At the top of the staircase leading to the lower deck she ran into Noel Frensham. She had not expected to see him up, because last night he seemed to be in more pain than usual. But here he was. He looked a bad colour, with dark shadows under his eyes, and Peta could have sworn that the white drill suit was hanging loosely on him, as though he had gone to skin and bone. Yes, he was a very sick man just making an effort to get about, pitting his will-power against the increasing weakness of his flesh. When he smiled and greeted her, she felt the effort

23

behind the smile.

'Here we are at Aden,' he said.

'Ought you to be up?' asked Peta.

He shrugged his shoulders.

'Possibly not. I feel like hell. But what's the good of staying in bed? Infernally hot, and dull into the bargain.'

'Seen the doctor this morning?'

'No; I've stopped wasting his time and mine. I know as much about myself as he does.'

'Well, come and sit down,' said Peta.

He did not take much persuading. His legs felt weak under him, his head was dizzy, and there was always that pain which baffled both him and the other medical man. God! he thought as he sank into a deck-chair under the awning—it was as close up on deck as down in the cabin. Or was it his imagination? His temples felt as though steel bands were compressing them. He wished he knew what was wrong, and, above all things, he wished that he was at home.

He looked out of his sunken eyes at the girl who was regarding him so anxiously. A kind little thing, he thought. She had been sweet to sit with him so often. This strange sickness which consumed him made him feel horribly depressed, unlike himself. And lonely, too—a thing he had never felt in his life before. The days had seemed long and the nights even longer. He had begun to look forward to the moments when Peta Marley sat beside him. It made him forget himself to listen to her talk and hear all her youthful aspirations and philosophies. Such a lovely, ardent child! At the very beginning of things! The five days at sea had brought a warm rose as well as the tan to her face, and instead of wasting away like himself, her cheeks had filled out. She looked deliciously well and full of vitality. Nothing much wrong with her! He said:

'Going on shore? There's a fine bathing-place at Aden, you know, and everybody goes to the club for lunch.'

Peta shook her head.

'I don't want to. You won't be going, will you?'

'Heavens, no. I couldn't put one foot in front of the other.'

'Then I shall stay and talk to you.'

'Nonsense. There's no earthly reason why you should. Get one of the young men to take you ashore.'

'I assure you I don't want to go ashore with any of the young men,' she said. 'You need a nurse to look after you, Dr. Frensham, and I'm going to be that nurse. I don't believe you're eating anything, and you ought to have somebody strong-minded enough to keep you in your bed.'

He gave a faint smile, then shut his eyes because the blinding morning light hurt them so.

'Don't bully me,' he said. 'I'll be a lamb and

25

do exactly as Nurse Marley suggests, but I won't lie in that cabin. It's an inferno.'

'So's mine,' she said. 'I do sympathise, really. Now what about breakfast?'

But he would have nothing to eat. He only wanted a drink. Peta, herself, poured him out a cup of coffee and took it up to him. After he had drunk it he seemed to doze. She stole away and ate her own breakfast, and then returned with a book and sat beside him. His eyes were still shut. How thin and grey his face looked, she thought. In repose it was a very fine face, strongly moulded, yet sensitive. She wondered what on earth *was* wrong with him. It must be ghastly to be ill on a ship and not know the cause.

All through that day at Aden, most of the passengers went ashore, but Peta stayed with the sick man. They talked very little. He seemed to doze a good deal. At sundown they left Aden and it grew cooler; then he sat up, smoked a cigarette, and made an effort to take some interest in what was going on around him. But Peta could see that he was really too ill to care.

She had to get the deck-steward to help Noel down to his cabin. He could not walk alone. That was a bad sign. He was definitely weaker. Peta felt driven to talk to the ship's doctor about Dr. Frensham that night.

She waylaid him as they were coming out of the dining saloon.

26

'I've been sitting with Dr. Frensham,' she said. 'I've had a little hospital experience, and it worries me to see him growing worse instead of better. What do you think?'

The ship's doctor was a mere boy. It was his first journey and he was not very inspired. He murmured something about 'a bad form of malaria and some indication of appendicitis,' and that was as much as Peta could get out of him. He was doing all he could, of course. Peta said that she was sure of that and passed on, feeling no happier about Noel.

When she went to the cabin to say good night to the man whom she had begun to look upon in the light of a special patient, she found him in a state of complete dejection.

'I believe I'm for the sharks,' he told Peta.

'You're not to say such a thing,' she said in a shocked voice.

He moved his head wearily on the pillow.

'It wouldn't matter much to anybody.'

'That's wicked of you,' said Peta severely. 'There are plenty of people who'd be frightfully upset, and you know it. All your patients, for instance.'

Frensham's features twisted into a grin. He let his dark, dulled gaze rest on her for an instant.

'Our little romancist! But you can't weave a romance about me. I've walked alone for many years, and I assure you if I passed out, it would be a financial benefit rather than a sad loss.'

'Don't say things like that,' said Peta, 'it upsets me; honestly it does.'

Impulsively he put out a hand and she placed hers in it. She noticed how dry and hot his thin fingers were.

'You're a kind child,' he murmured, 'and I didn't mean to tease you.'

Peta blushed a little.

'I know you think I'm awfully romantic.'

'Perhaps you're wise to be. There's little of real romance in the world, but I'd be sorry if you let your imagination be captured by the wrong ideas—the wrong person.'

She drew her hand away rather quickly.

'Why do you say that?'

'I've been thinking about this man you sometimes speak of. You're staking a lot on him, aren't you? I'd hate you to be disillusioned —when you get home.'

'Why should I be? He told me he loved me. Why shouldn't I believe him?'

'But he didn't ask you to marry him. I should have liked it better if he had.'

Peta looked down at the tips of her fingers with their rose-tinted nails. Fingers that Auburn had kissed and crushed so feverishly. Why hadn't he asked her to marry him? Why had he just made wild love to her and talked about 'when we get back to London'? After all, why should he propose to her in London any more than in Calcutta? Dr. Frensham was right. But she didn't want to think it. Her heart failed her at the very idea that Auburn might let her down. She loved him so very much. Her very fear made her say angrily:

'You have no right to suggest that . . . *he* isn't as serious as I am.'

'Sorry, my dear,' said Noel Frensham. 'Of course I had no right to suggest it.'

Immediately Peta was mollified.

'Oh, but you had,' she said. 'I asked you to tell me what you thought, Dr. Frensham. You may be right. I can only hope you aren't. Oh, I do hope it, because, you see . . .'

'Because you're very much in love,' he finished for her quietly. 'Yes, I do see, and from the bottom of my heart I wish you the best of luck.'

Tears were stinging Peta's eyes, and she drew the back of her hand across them like an embarrassed boy.

'You should go to sleep,' she said, 'not bother about my affairs. I'll say good night.'

He wondered ironically how much sleep he was going to get. Wasn't he in for another of these damnably long, almost terrifying nights when he lay wide awake hour after hour wondering if he would ever be free from pain or look upon his native land again! Queer things, these sea voyages. One never knew when one stepped on the boat what was waiting at the other end. For him perhaps there would be nothing . . . only an ending of another kind. And for this girl with her slim grace, her soft dark eyes, and intense nature ... there might be the bitterness of an unrequited love . . . or, if the fellow was all that she believed, the passionate arms of a lover who meant to marry her. That was what Noel Frensham hoped for Peta. It was strange how attached he had grown to her, how interested during these five days at sea. He wouldn't like her to be hurt.

His heavy eyes closed. Peta thought that he was asleep and tiptoed out of the cabin. He let her go. Perhaps she would go on deck and dance and be happy. It wasn't fair to keep her down here when he was sick and depressed. Yet his heart sank as he heard her go. He felt so ill. He would like to have had little Peta Marley's hand to hold ... to know that she was there beside him, with all her sweetness and compassion. He switched off the light above his bed and lay, hot, restless, in pain, listening to the swish-swish of the water as the boat ploughed through the moonlit sea towards Port Said.

CHAPTER FOUR

Never in her life was Peta to forget that journey through the Suez Canal. Most of the passengers spent those four days from Aden to Port Said sitting on deck enjoying the scenery.

There was so much to be seen. Endless miles of desert sands on one side, lovely cultivated land on the other. A stream of boats, smoke-grey, white, and the beautiful coloured feluccas of the Nile, passing up and down the narrow Canal. Life, colour, glamour, and always the splendid blue of the Eastern sea and sky.

But Peta missed it all. For Noel Frensham was worse, and she spent most of her time below in his cabin. Being the only woman on board with hospital experience, she had been asked by the ship's doctor to help take charge of the case until they got to Port Said. If Dr. Frensham was no better when they reached the Port, he would have to be taken off, Peta was told, and carried into hospital.

The night before they docked was one of the worst Noel had had. His whole body seemed on fire and raging with pain. At intervals the fever reached such a pitch that he was delirious. And now Peta found herself in for some hard nursing. Wearing a white overall borrowed from the stewardess, with sleeves rolled up, she worked with the doctor to bring down the sick man's temperature. Bathing, ice-packs, bathing again. And in between the attacks, Peta, exhausted, sat beside Noel's bed, looking with pity at the gaunt, wasted body, at the face which had grown bony and waxen with a dark stubble of beard. He was a wreck of the debonair man who had come on board at Bombay. A man who, when he was conscious,

31

was so weak that he could only open his dark, sunken eyes and whisper his thanks before he dropped into a semi-conscious state again.

That night Peta, her whole body dripping with the heat and her eyes weighted with lack of sleep, learned how strangely intimate one can become with a very sick person whom one is nursing. Dr. Frensham was like her child, like the little Bradley boy whom she had helped nurse through a fever. That boy had clung to his mother, crying to her not to leave him. In just such a way Noel, unconscious of what he did or said, clung to Peta's hands during the night and would not let her go. And she wiped the sweat from his temples, put iced bandages across them, and kept his thin, hot wrist between her fingers, soothing him as though she were indeed his mother.

The ship's doctor complimented her. She was marvellous, he said. A pity she had not been strong enough to continue her hospital training. He snatched some sleep himself, just before dawn, and left Frensham in her hands. Before he went, Peta asked what he thought of Noel's chances. He shook his head and gave a non-committal reply. Dr. Frensham was very ill, he said, and there was no knowing which way things might go with him. Whatever this mysterious malady was, it had got the upper hand at the moment. At Port Said they would get other opinions.

When the ship docked at Port Said on that

32

brilliant morning, Noel Frensham became suddenly very clear-headed. He was firmly convinced that he was going to die. He told Peta so, and Peta tried in vain to dissuade him from that notion.

'They're going to take you off and get you into a hospital and make you quite well again,' she said, adopting a bright, professional voice. But there was a horrible lump in her throat as she looked down at him. In the night he had seemed old. This morning his face was strangely young and attractive in its transparency. His eyes were abnormally large and bright. They seemed to look straight into her soul. He smiled at her.

'You've been an angel to me,' he whispered. 'You don't know how grateful I am.'

She made an effort not to break down and cry.

'All I want is for you to get fit again.'

'I'm going to die,' he said, 'and before I die there's something I want you to do.'

Peta swallowed hard.

'Anything,' she said, and wished frantically that they'd hurry up and bring the stretcher and take him into hospital, where there would be medical men who understood his condition, and could stave off that sinister Shadow which she felt was lurking in this cabin, whilst outside Port Said lay vivid, colourful, noisy, and so very vital under the blazing sun.

Noel Frensham made a movement with his

hand, and she guessed that he wanted her to place her fingers in it, and did so.

'Peta,' he said in a thin, far-away voice, 'Peta, will you come on shore with me?'

'Of course, if you want me to.'

'Will you stay . . . *stay* with me . . .'

'You mean—let the boat go on without me?'

'Yes. Is it too much to ask? You can easily . . . pick up another . . . but I don't want you to leave me. It won't matter, will it? You can send a cable and explain. But it will mean . . . everything to me.'

For a moment she was too confused to think. Of course it wouldn't matter much whether she was a week late or not. The poor man needed her . . . yet what could she do? There would be proper nurses in the hospital. It was merely the sick fancy of a very sick man. She didn't want to refuse, and yet she didn't want to accept. She was anxious to get back . . . because of Auburn.

Noel Frensham's fingers tightened about her hand.

'Peta . . . please . . . don't leave me.'

She found it impossible to disappoint him. Perhaps he was, indeed, a dying man. She couldn't refuse a final request like that. What did it matter if she stayed a few days in Port Said? It would be horrible for him to die alone in a strange land. He was an English doctor and must have saved many lives and done much good. She would like to do something

34

for him. All that was generous in her urged her to accede to his strange wish.

And so it was that Peta Marley disembarked at Port Said and walked beside the stretcher on which Dr. Frensham was carried on land . . . a dying man, so it was rumoured amongst all the passengers.

Peta had little time in which to regret her hasty decision. She sent a wireless to the Bradleys from the ship, telling them that she had been detained at Port Said and would write an explanation. After that she was kept busy. Noel Frensham would not let her out of his sight. She went with him to the hospital and stayed there in the private room which had been prepared for him.

It was Peta who interviewed the doctors and members of the staff and told them all that had happened to Noel Frensham since he left Bombay, just as though she had been a relative. Just as though she was his wife, she told herself dryly. In fact, the matron had thought that she was his wife, or at least his fiancée, and had been a little frigid when Peta had explained that she was no more than a friend.

After two doctors, one English and one American, had made a thorough examination, they gave Peta their report. In their belief Noel Frensham was suffering from the effects of a microbe, possibly picked up in the jungle while he was on safari . . . which was exactly what

35

Noel himself had thought. They could put a name to it, and it could, in most cases, be cured, they told Peta. But they were afraid that the patient had come too late. The thing had gone too far. It was their opinion that Dr. Frensham could not last more than a couple of days, although, of course, they would do everything in their power to save him.

The news had a devastating effect upon Peta. She had never felt more unhappy. She could think of nothing but Noel and the tragedy of this untimely end to his brilliant career. She scarcely gave a thought to her own peculiar position in having let the boat go on without her, and landing herself at Port Said with only just enough money to exist upon until she picked up the next boat that called.

Nightfall found her still with Noel at the hospital. She was allowed to stay because the sick man grew worse when she left his side.

Peta was dead tired and horribly depressed. She had seen nothing of Port Said. The heat, the noise, the throbbing life of the place which has been called 'the wickedest city in the world' revolved unknown to her outside the quiet hospital walls.

She did not even know where she was going to sleep tonight. Her luggage was here. No doubt she would find an hotel later.

Late that evening, sitting by Noel's bed, she wondered how to keep her heavy eyelids open. She longed for a cigarette, but dared not light one here. Her nerves were jangling. Wearily she looked down at Noel Frensham, who lay so still and mask-like on his white pillow. They had just given him an injection. And in two days he would be gone, she reflected dismally . . . buried out here with no one but herself to mourn for him. The tragedy of it smote Peta's tender heart. She found herself crying quietly for this man whom she had nursed and taken care of and whose name, just over a week ago, she had not even known.

Noel Frensham opened his eyes and saw Peta sitting there with the tears pelting down her cheeks. He knew that she was crying for him, and it filled him with inexpressible tenderness for her.

'Don't, my dear . . .' he whispered, 'you mustn't be sorry because I . . .'

But she wouldn't let him finish.

'You're going to get well,' she said. 'You've *got* to get well.'

'But they've told you,' he said, 'there's no hope.'

'No, no! They may be wrong.'

'But they may be right. You've done so much, Peta . . . but there's one more thing I'm going to ask you to do.'

She put her hand gently over his.

'What is it?'

'I want you to marry me.'

For a moment she was stupefied. Then she gave a short, embarrassed laugh.

'Dr. Frensham!'

'It may sound fantastic, but I mean it . . . I want you to marry me before I die . . . you can arrange it. Go, see the British Consul now, at once, and arrange it . . . before it's too late.'

Her cheeks were red as poppies.

'But it's impossible.'

'Not if you'll do it. Oh, I know you don't want to marry me and that you're in love with this other man, but it's not going to spoil your chances with him. If anything it will enhance them. I shall leave you everything. I'm a rich man and you'll benefit. It'll mean nothing more to you than bearing my name.'

Peta put a hand to her heart, which was thudding at a ridiculous pace. Noel Frensham couldn't be in his right mind to make such a suggestion. She tried to argue, to protest, but he was insistent, and, indeed, seemed quite clear in his mind as to what he wanted. He explained that his sole heir at the moment was his cousin Kenneth, who was a wretched youth to whom he did not wish to leave five thousand a year and the rest of his possessions.

He would much rather leave them to her, he said. She had nothing—nobody. He would like to make her independent. She need never feel that she had to work again or that she had to marry, unless she wanted to. He implored her to do it. Once she was his wife, everything that he had in the world would automatically become hers.

By the terms of his father's will the money must remain in the family. It would have been simple, could he have made a will and left everything to her, but that wasn't possible. If he died unmarried, everything would pass to the next of kin. That was why he must make her his wife.

'It *can't* hurt you, Peta,' he persisted feebly, but with determination, 'and it will make me die happy. I've grown so fond of you, child. Let me die knowing that what I leave will become yours.'

Her protests were silenced by his repeated and urgent pleading that she should accept his offer. Her thoughts were chaotic. It couldn't be right . . . and yet, of course, when she considered it, it *would* be marvellous to be independent. Five thousand a year . . . good heavens, it was a fortune! And there was one big temptation. She felt that if she had money of her own it would put her on an equal footing with Auburn Lyell. She could meet him on his own ground. It would make things right between them. Then another thought struck her. Supposing by any chance Noel Frensham lived? Then they would all be in a nice mess.

Frensham seemed to read that thought, because now he was saying:

'If by any miracle I survive, I give you my word that the marriage will be annulled, if you wish it, so you'll be no worse off than you were before.'

She could feel his fingers hot, trembling in hers. His sunken eyes went on beseeching her.

'Do this for me, Peta. I hate to die and feel that I have achieved nothing. To leave you my wife with all my possessions would make me feel so very happy.'

He broke off and lay gasping, livid. She was terrified that he was going to die now and rang quickly for the nurse. But he still had strength to go on pleading. Peta, worn down, and caring very little what did happen, found herself accepting that amazing proposal. Breathlessly, half reluctantly and quite dizzily—she promised to marry Noel Frensham before he died.

CHAPTER FIVE

The British Consul at Port Said came to the hospital at an early hour that next morning and in the presence of two witnesses, a doctor and nurse, married Peta Marley to Noel Frensham.

Peta was so nervous and confused during that hastily arranged ceremony, that she could hardly speak the words requested of her, and when she did say 'I will,' it seemed too incredible to be true. She had read in newspapers and books about 'deathbed marriages,' but little had she expected to find herself in a leading role as the bride. And how frightening it was to think that a marriage ceremony could be performed at a moment's notice like this—binding two people together, altering the whole of their lives. There had been no difficulty about it. Just a hasty interview with the Consul, a special licence, and it was all over.

It was her hand that trembled when the Consul joined her fingers to those of Noel. His grasp was weak, yet steady. He had just sufficient strength to put the ring on her finger that narrow gold band purchased by herself. And when she dared look at the man whom she was marrying, his sunken eyes were calm. Only hers were full of panic. She felt panic-stricken. She had begun to regret the promise she had made to the sick man almost as soon as she started to carry it out, but felt she could not draw back, once having promised.

How long would he live? That was the main question burning in her mind during that marriage, and afterwards, when doctors and nurses were congratulating her. One or two romantic-minded of the nursing staff brought in flowers, and even a glass of champagne was offered by a young doctor who thought the bride 'darned pretty,' and pitied the unlucky fellow who had married her and wasn't going to live.

All through that day Noel lingered. For the most part he was semi-conscious. But

41

sometimes his eyes opened and he whispered Peta's name. He seemed more content when he found her there beside him, ready to place her hand in his and murmur some soothing word.

That same afternoon Peta still felt that she was in some kind of fantastic dream, and that she must eventually wake up to find herself in her cabin on a ship that was making fast headway for Marseilles. That she would laugh at herself, at the discovery that she was still Peta Marley and that Dr. Frensham was just a fellow passenger with whom she had made friends.

But no! It was not a dream. Here she was in the hospital with a certificate in her bag which gave her the right to call herself Mrs. Noel Frensham. The right, as Noel had reminded her after their marriage, to receive the full benefits as his widow when she reached England again.

At the moment she did not want to think about England or any of those benefits. She felt that it would be hardly decent to allow herself to dwell upon the fact that Noel's death would open for her the gates to a world in which she had never so far lived. A world of money, luxury, independence, everything that she could reasonably desire.

She couldn't think about it whilst Noel Frensham was still gasping here in his bed. She liked him. She didn't want him to die. Yet obviously they would both find themselves in a nice tangle if he lived. Best not to think about it at all. Just sit here and wait. But of course it isn't always possible to chase away thoughts, and a confusion of them kept flitting wildly through Peta's brain hour after hour as the long day went on.

An unbelievable day! After lunch, one of the doctors insisted upon her snatching some sleep, because it was written all over her, he said, that she would collapse if she did not take a rest. So for a few hours she had lain down in one of the nurses' bedrooms. But she could not sleep for long. By teatime she was back again at Noel Frensham's side.

'Your husband seems easier when you are with him,' the nurses told her.

Her husband! That, of course, just sounded mad and not true. How could she have consented to such craziness? She didn't know Noel. He was a stranger and not the man she wanted to marry. She was in love with Auburn Lyell. She wondered chaotically what Auburn would say if he knew what had happened to her since she left Bombay. Of course, he must not know until she could explain, or he might imagine she was just incapable of being faithful to a man's memory for longer than a week! She would have to keep this news a dead secret until she could give Auburn, and everyone else she knew, a personal account of what had happened and why she had

43

consented to this marriage.

Why had she done it? She wasn't at all sure. Now that it was over and she realised what she had done, she could see no very definite reason for it. Just that she had been sorry for Noel and anxious to make him happy before he died, and, of course, she was human enough to have been tempted by what the marriage implied. No girl would turn down such an offer unless she was an idiot. What impecunious nursery-governess could fail to welcome the prospect of becoming a 'widow' with a handsome income and no responsibilities?

Would the day never end? Hour after hour keeping this vigil, waiting for Noel to open his heavy eyes and call her name . . . waiting for the end that the doctors said must come tonight.

Hour after hour of the close, oppressive atmosphere in the hospital. It was hot despite all efforts to maintain a cool, even temperature. Outside, Port Said gasped under a remorseless sun.

There seemed a constant flow of people into the little private ward. More doctors, including a famous Egyptian who was reputed to have effected marvellous cures. Endless examinations and discussions and whisperings about the patient. Medicines, injections, ice packs to bring down his temperature, special nurses. The whole hospital seemed to be concentrating upon the sick English doctor

44

who had been carried off the boat, and whose case was extraordinary. He aroused much interest, because his name was known so well in the British medical world.

Special interest was shown in Peta, too, because she was young and pretty and had been romantically married to the dying man at a moment's notice. Everything was done that could be done. So many things, in fact, that Peta lost count of them, and grew weary of saying: 'Thank you so much.' And every time somebody called her 'Mrs. Frensham,' it sent cold shivers down her spine and brought her sharply face to face with realities.

She tried to write to Auburn, but failed. She couldn't write this news. She *must* wait to see him. She tore up the letter. She started another to an aunt, a sister of her mother's living in Devonshire, and married to a gentleman farmer. Peta, as a small girl, had spent many holidays down there on the farm, and was fond of her aunt. But she tore up that letter too. She could imagine with what horror Aunt Annie and Uncle Bob would receive the news that their niece had been married in a Port Said hospital to an entire stranger! A well-known physician he might be, but that wouldn't make it any better in Auntie Annie's eyes. She was of the generation that liked a proper announcement of a proper engagement, followed by a proper lapse of time until a nice little wedding in the parish church was performed.

Peta would have to write to the Bradleys, too, she reflected. They would be staggered by her cable, and possibly anxious into the bargain. But she just could not put pen to paper today, so she gave up trying. She could cable to the Bradleys again tomorrow.

The hours dragged by.

At seven o'clock that evening Noel Frensham came out of the dark phantom world in which he had been drifting and became conscious of the room in which he was lying, and of the girl who sat by his side. A girl in a grey flannel suit and white blouse with a tired, worried young face in a frame of dark ruffled curls. Her slim hands nervously turned over the pages of a magazine which she was not attempting to read.

Noel Frensham knew what he had done. He had married this girl. She was his wife. He was going to die and then she would be his widow and all that belonged to him would be hers.

A great gladness came over him. At the same time it was a queer feeling . . . to know that he, who had been sworn to bachelorhood and work for thirty-nine years, should pass out of this life a married man. Married to a girl whom he had only known just over a week.

He remembered his first meeting with Peta when he had felt so confoundedly ill and she had given him that glass of water in the cabin. He had thought he was going to share the cabin with a Mr. Peter Marley. And she had laughed and told him that her name was Peta.

Peta Mary. That was what she had signed on the marriage certificate. Now she was Peta Mary Frensham. He was glad. His mother's name had been Mary. It sounded right. There had been other Mary Frenshams in the family, too. But never a Peta. How would she like the Wimpole Street house? It might appear gloomy to her, perhaps. A little overwhelming. But she would adore the Lodge on the Scottish moors.

He lay still, quietly visualising Peta in tweeds and brogues, tramping with his dogs through the heather, the curling Autumn mists against her brown young face. It would suit her up there. She liked the country and animals. She had told him so.

He hoped she wouldn't marry that fellow whom she had met in Calcutta. He sounded rather a cad. Still—if she loved him and would be happy, what did anything else matter? Some fellow, anyhow, must inevitably possess all that youth and sweetness which would never be his, Noel's. He wondered had he known her under other circumstances, if he would have fallen in love with her? Hard to tell. But he could well believe that she would be adorable in a man's arms. And he felt quite absurdly jealous and annoyed to think that he was passing out, leaving her for another.

Peta turned her head and met his gaze.

47

Immediately she put down the magazine and said:

'Are you all right? Do you want anything?'

'Nothing,' he said in his weak, thin voice. But she sensed that he craved for her hand, and she placed her fingers in his, noticing as she did so that his fingers were cooler. She placed the other hand on his forehead. It was damp, but, like his hand, cooler to the touch than it had been recently. How terribly large and sad his eyes seemed in his wasted face! So sad that they hurt. She could not bear such sadness. She said:

'Oh, I wish I could do something for you!'

He smiled.

'Haven't you done enough? Peta, I've been thinking . . . I'm not only sorry to be leaving this life and my work and all that I know and love . . . but sorry to leave you.'

The colour flooded her face and throat. She felt very embarrassed. But she smiled back at him and said:

'That's nice of you. But hush, don't speak about leaving this life.'

His lips gave a wry twist.

'It'd be mighty aggravating for you, my child, if I . . . fooled 'em all and got through.'

Peta swallowed hard. She could think of no answer to that. She felt unutterably confused.

'I . . . I'd better ring for your nurse.'

Weakly his fingers clung to hers.

'You don't regret . . . marrying me?'

48

'No, of course not.'

'I hope you'll like all my things.'

She felt that she was going to choke.

'Of course, of course I will.'

His breath came more quickly as though he had found talking an effort.

'Take special care of . . . Jonnie.'

'Who is he?'

'My pet dog up in Scotland. My Cairn terrier.'

'Of course. I'll love him. I love all dogs.'

His eyes closed for a moment. The effort of talking exhausted him. But soon his lashes lifted and he looked at her again.

'Peta, do you think . . . you'll marry this man you told me about?'

She was scarlet now. Her ears were burning. And her very heart twisted at the thought of marriage with Auburn Lyell. If only he were here or could come to her to help her through this shattering affair! What wouldn't she have given to feel his arms about her and hear that gay, charming voice of his saying absurdly charming things as only Auburn knew how!

She heard Noel's panting voice:

'Tell me . . . answer me . . .'

'Oh, I don't know!' she stammered. 'Honestly I don't.'

'You want to marry him?'

'I—I suppose so.'

Frensham gave a long sigh. His expression grew remote, resigned. Why should it matter to him if she wanted to marry another man? He was beyond all that sort of thing now. And very soon he would be shut away in a cold grave in that grim cemetery in Port Said. He remembered seeing it on his last trip and thinking how grim it was! Little had he thought that he would end up there, and before he was forty!

Peta was stroking his hand with her kind, friendly fingers, telling him not to talk any more, but to rest and reserve his strength. And suddenly resignment to death vanished and in its place came a terrific and uncontrollable wish to live. To go on with his absorbing career, that work in the medical world which had always been his first, his last thought. To be able to walk about again fit and strong and ready for anything that came his way. To eat, to sleep, to wake refreshed, to see the beauty of sunrise and sunset; to look upon his favourite books and pictures, hear outside his house the roar of traffic; drive his car down Piccadilly at night; see the flashing illuminations in dear old London. To tramp his beloved moors and watch Jonnie's small, wheaten-coloured body careering madly after a rabbit. To come back to a peat fire and smoke a pipe. To come back to *her*, maybe, this girl, Peta, who was young and sweet and his wife. *God!* to know that she was his wife and that they were lovers.

His face suddenly contorted with the

vehemence of his thoughts and he tried to raise his head from the pillow.

'No! No!' he gasped.

'Oh, what is it?' asked Peta.

'I don't . . . *I don't want to die, Peta.*'

Agonised for him and by him, she put an arm about his shoulders and tried to give him comfort.

'No, of course you don't. Perhaps you won't. Oh, Dr. Frensham! . . .'

She broke off, incoherently, choking, hardly realising that she had committed the absurdity of addressing her husband as Dr. Frensham, and that she was telling him that he mustn't die, and yet she had only married him *because* he was dying. Really, it was too much for her. More than she could stand. She pushed him gently back on the pillow and rang for a nurse.

The nurse did not like the patient's colour. It was bad, she said. Maybe this was the end. She went for Dr. Lane, the senior physician who was mainly in charge of the case. Noel lay motionless, waxen. And Peta stood a little way from the bed with both clenched hands pressed against her cheeks, battling with a wild desire to break down and sob.

'I don't want to die, Peta!'

She wondered if she would ever forget that sudden cry which had had all of mortal terror, anguish and human feeling in it.

The room seemed to fill with people. Somebody was leading her away. She began to

51

cry hysterically:

'Is he dead? Is he?'

A nurse answered:

'No. Dr. Lane is with him. They're going to give oxygen. Don't cry, my dear. Come and sit down in our sitting-room. It's all been too much for you.'

She allowed herself to be led to the nurses' room. She was given a cup of tea with a dash of brandy in it, and she drank it with the tears pouring down her cheeks and wished childishly and desolately that somehow she could get in touch with Auburn because she was so miserable. Nobody but Auburn could make her any better.

At the end of half an hour she was told that Noel still breathed and that she must not give up hope. The matron suggested that she should take a sleeping-draught and lie down again, otherwise she would make herself ill. They would send for her, the matron said, if Dr. Frensham called for her, and they saw that the end had come.

Was that end going to come? Her eyes asked that question dumbly. The matron was non-committal, although more sympathetic than she had been in the first place, now that there had been a marriage and she knew that she was dealing with a well-known doctor's wife.

Peta took that sleeping-draught and went back to bed in the nurses' room which had been lent to her. The dope on top of her own exhaustion acted speedily and she fell into the deepest and most dreamless sleep she had ever known.

She woke to find that it was night again and lights were burning, and someone gently shaking her. She sat up, rubbing her eyes, and saw a sister and Dr. Lane himself standing beside her. Immediately her thoughts flew to Noel.

'Is it all over?'

The sister took one of her hands and patted it.

'No, no, it isn't over. We have good news for you.'

And Dr. Lane, looking tired but pleased, smiled and nodded down at her.

'The happiest news, Mrs. Frensham. Almost a miracle, in fact. Since that last attack of your husband's, we have noticed a marked improvement in his condition. You know we have been doing everything in our power to fight that infernal microbe and clear his body of poison. We didn't think he stood a chance. But he has a wonderful constitution and he's helped himself. This afternoon he seemed to take on a new lease of life as though he were making a big effort to live. Well, of course, he is still a very sick man, but I am happy to be able to tell you that there is now every chance of his recovery.'

Peta stared up at him. For a moment her

mind was a blank.

She could do nothing but stare. She heard the sister add:

'Isn't that wonderful? He's been sleeping for the last few hours just as you have, and his pulse is much more normal. We're going to give him something to drink in a minute. Would you like to come along and see him?'

Peta put a trembling hand to her lips. What they were telling her was soaking through to her brain now. Noel wasn't dead and wasn't any longer dying. He was going to get well. She was glad about that, of course. But there was no getting away from the fact that she would pay now for the risk she had taken in marrying him. He was alive and she remained his wife.

She began to laugh loudly and hysterically, the tears streaming down her cheeks. The sister looked shocked. The doctor murmured something about giving her sal volatile. Naturally it had all been a great strain. He went out and left her with the woman, who nearly drove Peta to distraction by her continual reiteration of the name 'Mrs. Frensham.'

'Lucky girl, Mrs. Frensham,' she said. 'Your man will pull through, and you'll be able to go back to England and have your honeymoon after all.'

Honeymoon! That sent icy little chills up and down Peta's spine. Oh, this was awful and she ought never to have consented to this marriage, never! She might have known that things would go this way. Of course, Noel had said that if he lived they would annul the marriage. But it would take time, and might have to be made public, and oh, *what* would Auburn say?

The thought of Auburn turning from her with indifference, taking it for granted that she had no interest in him, was too shattering.

Somehow or other she managed to pull herself together, dry her eyes, powder her face, and accompany the sister to Noel's room.

'The sight of you will do him a lot of good,' the wellmeaning woman said in her bright, professional voice. 'Dear Dr. Frensham! We're all so glad that he's taken this miraculous turn for the better. And glad for you, too, my dear. It's wonderful for you both.'

Peta, her heart sinking as she walked into the private ward, wondered just how wonderful it was going to be.

CHAPTER SIX

Frensham's first words to Peta when she stood beside his bed were typical of his dry, rather cynical wit with which she was beginning to be familiar.

He opened his eyes, cocked an eyebrow, and whispered:

'Sorry I'm still alive, my dear. It looks as though I've fooled them all—or they've fooled me—'

She stood silent. She was trembling. It was on the tip of her tongue to say:

'I'm the one that's been fooled.'

But that wouldn't be kind or even decent when a man had come through from the shadow of death, no matter how serious the consequences of this 'deathbed marriage' might be.

She managed to say:

'That's all right—you couldn't help it, could you? . . .' And then she laughed hysterically.

Frensham's eyes half closed again, shutting out the sight of her face. He didn't like to see it like that, distorted, pale and afraid. He still felt so very ill. Even if they were sure now of his recovery, he could see that there was a lot of trouble in store for him. He had loathed the thought of dying, but this was a devilish mess, all right. He had married this child in order to leave her his possessions, knowing quite well that she wanted to marry somebody else.

He looked at her again.

'Very sorry, Peta. Meant to make you my widow—not my wife.'

She put a hand against her lips and tried to stop trembling.

'Please don't go on apologising for . . . for not dying!' she implored, and had never felt so overwrought in her life.

She was terrified that at any moment she would burst into tears and laughter combined.

'Tough for you, my dear, but if I don't peg out . . . and they say I won't . . . we'll get an annulment.'

She wanted to ask a dozen questions. Could they annul the marriage here? Must there be lengthy legal proceedings? Must there be publicity in England? Oh, so many things she wanted to know, but kindness forbade that she should harry a still very sick man with a lot of selfish questions. She sat down limply by the bed.

'It's all right. Please don't worry about anything for the moment, Dr. Frensham.'

That brought a smile to his lips. He felt hazy, tired and monstrously weak. He said:

'Seeing that we are married for the moment . . . can't I be . . . Noel to you?'

'Of course,' she laughed. She, too, was tired, and thankful when he put out a hand, gave hers a reassuring pat and whispered:

'Go to bed . . . talk to me in the morning . . . you must be done in.'

'I am tired,' she admitted, 'and you must sleep as well.'

'Promise you won't worry yourself. I won't let you down, little Peta. You've been so kind to me.'

The inclination to cry proved too strong for Peta. She put a handkerchief to her lips and rushed out of the room, weeping. In the corridor she collided with the sister in charge of the Frensham case. The woman firmly put an arm around the distraught young figure and piloted her off to bed.

'You're going to stay here another night with us, Mrs. Frensham, and not bother about hotels. Now don't cry, my dear. I know it's been an awful strain, but you can smile now because we've pulled your nice husband through.'

Peta felt that she would go quite mad if she heard those words, 'Mrs. Frensham' or 'husband,' any more.

Only when she was in bed in a nurse's vacant room, and it was quiet and dark and she was alone, could she calm down and feel able to think straight.

Well, why make all this fuss anyhow? She had brought trouble on herself when she had agreed to marry Noel Frensham, although, of course, everybody had led her to believe that there was no possible hope for him. It was so awful to feel half sorry that someone hadn't died. She *didn't* feel sorry that he hadn't died. She liked and admired him. She was glad he would live. Only she didn't want to be married to him!

She tried to comfort herself with the thought that he was the sort of person to be true to his word. He had said he wouldn't let her down, and he wouldn't. They would just annul the whole thing.

It would not be so worrying if it wasn't for

Auburn. But she didn't quite see how she could keep from him the fact that she *was* by law, anyhow, Noel Frensham's wife, and had no longer the right to call herself Miss Marley. The best thing to do would be to write a long letter to Auburn and tell him the whole strange story. She had the address of his Club in London. He lived in his father's house in Belgravia, but he was at the Club every day, he had said, and a letter would always reach him there. If he had left Calcutta by air, as he had intended, he should be in London now. She ought to write at once in case he carried out his half promise of meeting the boat at Tilbury. She decided to send a letter off by airmail in the morning.

She got up and wrote that letter at an early hour. She had slept soundly, but she was heavy eyed and anxious, and when she read the six closely written sheets, she was dissatisfied with them. It was all so awkward. There was no real understanding between herself and Auburn Lyell. He had told her that he loved her. And she knew that she was in love with him. But it seemed absurd under the circumstances to write and say:

'Dear Auburn,
'I've done something quite mad. I married an English doctor off the boat. He was supposed to be dying, but pulled through, and now I'm in a mess . . . !'

59

It might appeal to Auburn's sense of humour, but if he cared for her the news would be both a shock and a disappointment. He might just wish her luck and tell her to count him out of it. Awful thought! But the letter must go.

She paid a visit to her 'husband' before she posted the letter. There was a marked improvement in Frensham this morning. His temperature was right down and he was taking food. His voice when he bade Peta good morning was stronger, too.

'The whole thing seems a miracle,' he told her. 'That Egyptian fellow is a wizard with the injections. I actually had no pain last night. Of course it will take some time to get the poison out of my system, but they tell me I should be up in a fortnight's time.'

Peta avoided his gaze and looked nervously at one of his thin, sensitive hands.

'That's wonderful news,' she said.

'Damned aggravating for you, all the same.'

Her cheeks flamed. He thought, rather wistfully, how pretty she looked with that poppy colour under the tan. She was altogether attractive in her grey flannel suit, with a panama on the side of her dark curls. So young—almost schoolgirlish. It filled him with tenderness for her. When she moved her left hand he caught the flash of the gold wedding-ring, and thought how incredible it was that she should be his wife. He wished that he was more attractive to her. He wished that there hadn't been this other fellow. Yes, he had even grown to wish that there was no need to annul the marriage. Not that he was definitely in love, but something about Peta charmed him, and, during the long painful hours of his sickness, he had come definitely to the conclusion that it was by no means good for any man to live alone. He needed a wife and companion. He sighed heavily. There was all this annulment business to be discussed and arranged. Obviously she was in a panic about it and he had better put her mind at rest.

'Peta,' he said, 'I don't feel quite strong enough to discuss our affairs at length this morning. Give me another day, will you, child? But—'

'Of course you mustn't worry about it until you're miles better,' she broke in.

'But *you've* got to stop worrying,' he went on.

'I—I'm all right.'

'Look at me, Peta.'

She obeyed, and as her gaze met his, she felt absurdly embarrassed.

'You're scared to death, you poor little thing,' he murmured, 'but there's no need. You were damned good to me when I was so ill and I shan't forget it. I'm not going to claim my "rights" or anything like that, you know. So you needn't look like a bird in a snare.'

She blushed scarlet again and felt suddenly much better for what he said. She said in a softer voice:

'I swear I won't think anything of the sort. Just go on getting well and don't worry about anything.'

'You're very kind. But that's *you*.'

'You were kind to me. You meant it all for the best,' she stammered.

'It would have been all right if I'd done what was expected of me,' he whispered; 'you'd have had everything.'

And, he thought, he would still try and give her something—make her take some sort of allowance, just as though she had been his wife for a long time.

One of the doctors put an end to their conversation. The patient was doing well, but he was by no means well yet and must be kept very quiet, he said. Mrs. Frensham could stay with him, as long as she did not talk too much.

'Mrs. Frensham' decided that she would like to go out. She escaped speedily from the room, went out of the hospital and down to the town.

Another blazing day was beginning. Port Said sweltered under the sun. The harbour looked like blue glass and the light dazzled one's eyes. Peta did not really know where she was going, except that she wanted to post her letter to Auburn. She asked her way to the General Post Office and found herself in a street swarming with tourists, Europeans,

Arabs, Egyptians, men and women of all nationalities. Under happier circumstances it might have interested her, but she felt too confused and unhappy to enjoy sight-seeing, and the light and the noise made her head ache.

Noel would not be up and about for another fortnight. Would she have to stay in Port Said for these two weeks, or could she go home, she wondered? It would cause rather a scandal if she left the invalid who was supposed to be her newly-made bridegroom. That was the worst of it . . . the whole affair was so public and Noel Frensham so well-known in the medical world. She thought over what she had said in that letter which was in her bag, and wondered miserably how Auburn would take the news and if he would understand.

A couple of dark-skinned Egyptian boys wearing red fezes, with indescribably dirty faces, whined for alms and molested her all the way down the street, till at length in despair she turned into a large white building which looked like an hotel. People were drinking coffee on the verandah facing the sea. She could be at peace here for a moment and ask about the Air Mails to England.

As she walked into the cool vestibule, grateful for the shade and peace, a tall fair man wearing a white linen suit, strolled toward, her, examining some letters, which he held in his hand. Peta gave him a quick, amazed look. Then the blood rushed to her head. She gave a startled cry.

'*Auburn!*'

Auburn Lyell, the one man who had been in her thoughts so persistently since she left Calcutta, here in the flesh in this hotel! But what was he doing in Port Said? He had said he was flying to London. Peta almost fainted with excitement. Her spirits rose to their highest and she ran joyfully towards him.

'Burn!' she exclaimed, using the shortened name by which he was known to his familiar friends.

His head shot up. He dropped one of the letters he had been reading.

'Good God!' he said, '*Peta!*'

Shaking from head to foot she stood there looking up at him. It was too good to be true that Auburn Lyell should be here. The one person in the world she had wanted to see. It would be so much easier to tell him everything instead of leaving him to read an explanation which looked foolish in black and white.

'Peta,' he repeated, 'what in the name of fortune are you doing in Port Said?'

'I might say the same to you.'

'Well, I'm here on business, of course. I meant to go straight to London, but my father cabled out that I was to come here to meet a fellow who works for us in Cairo. I flew here, and I'm off again tomorrow. But you . . .what on earth made you leave the boat?'

'I can't tell you all in a minute. It's too . . . too fantastic,' she said with a little laugh.

He seized both her hands and squeezed them hard.

'It's a divine surprise anyhow,' he said. 'The best thing that's happened to me for a long time. Since I saw you off, I've had nothing but dull business meetings, cables, work —altogether too much work. I think I'm due for a little respite, and my Lord, Peta, seeing you . . . it's like a mirage in the desert.'

'Not a mirage,' she said happily, so unutterably happy she was, with her hands fast clasped in his, close to him, drinking in the passionate admiration which lay in his eyes. 'A mirage is something that doesn't exist. But I do, you know.'

'Thank the stars for that!'

'Are you really glad to see me, Burn?'

'Didn't I tell you in Calcutta,' he said, 'that you were the one and only girl for me?'

She thrilled from head to foot.

'Then you meant it.'

'My sweet, I always mean what I say. I meant it when I told you there could never be another woman now that I've met you.'

During which speech Auburn Lyell's tired, attractive eyes which held that subtly bad expression to which women respond so fatally, wandered over Peta's head about the lounge, whilst he hoped devoutly that that red-haired girl, Diana Something-or-other, with whom he had had a pretty hot flirtation last night, wouldn't appear at this precise moment.

'Come into the writing-room where we can be quiet and talk,' he added.

Peta went with him, and like any girl in love, prided herself on the fact that this man beside her was undeniably the most handsome and the most charming of his sex. She adored that crisp gold hair of his brushed smoothly back from his forehead, his tan, the blueness of his eyes and his big, amusing mouth. A weak mouth, a more experienced woman than Peta would have called it, and those long shaped eyes which were like the eyes of a sculptured faun, heavy lidded, and rather evil . . . they belonged, surely, to a man who had tasted evil and found it good, and who liked to take what was good and make it evil.

But Peta was very young and uninitiated and Auburn Lyell had drawn her into the net into which other women had fallen—and regretted it too late.

She was wildly happy to have found Auburn here in Port Said, and he was agreeably surprised. Little Peta Marley certainly attracted him. She was enchanting to look at and so sensitive and pliable. He liked girls to be that way. He was adept at playing on their emotions and fashioning their ideas to please his own.

When he had met her in Calcutta, he had felt that this was just what he had been looking for. His more recent affairs had not been very successful. There had been Val Porter, whose husband was one of the Lyell employees in Calcutta. Val had amused him vastly for some time, but he shied off that, because he didn't want to be involved in a divorce, and had no intention of marrying Val. Then there had been Philippa—the loveliest blonde he had known, and a marvellous dancer. They had had a big affair in London, but she was too sophisticated, was Phil, and had got to know him too well. It was boring for a man to realise that a woman knew his weak points. He had been rather 'off' affairs after the one with Phil ended, because there had been such a scene with her, and he loathed scenes. That was the worst of women. They would try to pin a chap down, even when they swore in the beginning that they realised it was only *'pour passer le temps.'* He had had the devil of trouble with Phil, and her letters, ranging from the pathetic to the infuriated, had only just ceased from arriving at his Club.

He wasn't going to get married. Not yet. He led a very pleasant life travelling about as a bachelor and living with parents who adored him and gave him everything that he wanted. The old man was a stickler for work and made Auburn do more than he fancied, but it was worth it and he had the hell of a good time alongside the business. There were few young men of his age, twenty-eight, who had as much money and as free a hand as the old man gave him.

He hadn't really meant to start an affair with the Bradleys' nursery-governess. But that rather sedate little air of hers, the real innocence—or should he call it lack of experience?—about her, had rather intrigued him. Added to which her large brown eyes were soft enough to weaken any man, and that long line of slender throat and the curve of her upper lip were most alluring.

When he had kissed her at the dance that night out in India, he had felt genuinely in love. He was very impressionable and he knew it. Things didn't last, but he could be serious for a time, and he had thought quite seriously about little Peta Marley. Besides, she was madly in love with him. There was an intensity in her which Phil had lacked. Phil had been after his money as much as himself. Peta wouldn't be like that, and every man likes to think that he is loved for himself alone.

There was something else about Peta which held Auburn Lyell, too. A remote streak. He felt that she wasn't quite as accessible as she appeared. Those sweet dark eyes of hers promised much. But she was not weak. There was strength in that small firm chin and he liked to have to fight for what he wanted. He knew it might be a fight between himself and Peta in the long run.

Peta was conscious of nothing but absurd

happiness when she sat on the sofa in the writing-room which they had to themselves, and Auburn's hand closed possessively over one of hers.

'I just can't get over this,' she said. 'Of all the people in the world—to meet you this morning—and I imagined you in England by now.'

'If I wasn't a modest man I'd take it for granted that you were pleased to see me,' he mocked her.

She mocked back at him:

'Modest man, indeed!'

'As a matter of fact I'm likely to have a swollen head at any minute if I can believe that you *are* pleased.'

A little pulse beat in her throat. This was the Auburn with whom she had fallen so madly in love out in Calcutta. The Auburn who could say the right thing in the right way. Such an insinuating way!

He lifted the small hand he was holding and put it against his cheek.

'Dear little Peta! And now you're going to tell me why *you* are here.'

Peta came down from the clouds and with a slight sense of shock remembered that letter in her bag and what she had written in it. Telling Auburn the truth wasn't going to be as easy as she had imagined. Especially as he was being so marvellous to her. It might drive him right away. It would be only natural, she thought, if

69

he declined to see any more of her, once he knew she was another man's wife—no matter what the circumstances of that marriage. She couldn't bear to lose Auburn because of it, and it wouldn't be fair. Besides, if Noel could set her free quickly and quietly, why tell Auburn at all? Or at least, why not wait to tell him when it was all over and she was free again?

She felt rather a coward about it, but she dreaded seeing that look of warmth, of feeling for her, fade from Auburn's handsome eyes. And while she sat there, hesitating, he gently pulled her close until she was resting her full weight against him. Then he murmured against her hair:

'What's it all about, little Peta? Are the Bradleys here too?'

Peta, her heart thumping crazily now that she was in his embrace, shut her eyes tightly and whispered:

'No. They went straight through to England on the boat before mine. Don't you remember?'

'Yes, I do. But why haven't you gone straight through as well?'

She wondered frantically what to do for the best and decided on a half-truth. She could tell him about Dr. Frensham without including that mad marriage which, after all, was going to be annulled. She could not, would not, risk sending Auburn away. She knew that he alone mattered in the world and that nobody else could matter in the same way.

Auburn put a finger under her chin and raised her face. He was intrigued by her silence and wondered what it was all about. Looking down into her eyes he read all the warmth and response in them that he wanted. And suddenly the sweetness and nearness of her went to his head and he did not care why she was in Port Said. He only knew that he was crazy about her—quite crazy, in fact. He caught her closer and kissed her full on the lips, and Peta's world rocked dizzily and dangerously for a second while she returned that kiss. One of her arms went round his neck. She heard him say:

'You're sweet. Lord, how sweet you are, Peta!'

She answered breathlessly:

'I love you, Burn. I love you.'

He kissed her again and again.

'I tried to make you say that in Calcutta and you wouldn't. Why wouldn't you?'

'Because I wasn't sure. I hardly knew you . . . but now . . .'

'Now are you sure, darling?'

Through the thick veil of her lashes she looked at him, flushed with that burning colour which enchanted him so. He had never known any other girl to blush in that adorable way.

'Now I am sure,' she said. 'I haven't thought of anything, anyone else since . . . since you saw me off on the boat train.'

71

'That's grand, Peta, because it's the same way with me.'

'But I don't know why . . . how . . . oh, Burn, are you certain?'

'Of course. Why shouldn't I be as certain as you are?'

'I . . . I don't know. But it seems so absurd that you should love me.'

'You're the least vain woman I've ever met, darling. Don't you realise how damned attractive you are?'

'Oh, I don't know,' she said, and buried her face in the crook of his arm.

He ruffled the dark curls which were thick and crisp about her small head. She was such a baby. That appealed vastly to his sophisticated fancy. He said:

'You're much too attractive. I think I'd better sit up and have a cigarette. You're making that heart of mine work overtime. And in this heat . . .'

He laughed, pulled a silk handkerchief from his pocket and passed it over his forehead. Peta sat up, too, powdered her nose and looked at him shyly, her eyes shining.

'It is hot,' she agreed, and laughed with him.

'Port Said, my dear. Loathly place. How about flying back to England with me this afternoon?'

She thought:

'Oh, if only I could!'

But she said nothing. She was remembering

the man who lay in that hospital on the hill, weak and ill and relying on her.

What a fool she had been! Why had she allowed herself to be swept by a cyclone of pity into that 'deathbed' marriage, with fatal results?

Auburn, tapping a cigarette on a thin gold case, looked at her through his long, rather womanish lashes, and said:

'Will you come with me, angel?'

'I can't,' she said, 'and you don't know why I'm here yet.'

'I've been too busy making love to you to care. And if I take you in my arms again, I still shan't care.'

'Oh, Burn,' she said, 'you make me feel I don't care either.'

'Then we're certainly in love,' he said, 'and we must certainly take that plane together.'

'We can hardly do that,' she said, the colour coming and going in her cheeks. 'We're not . . . we're not . . .'

'Not married, eh?' he finished for her.

She was silent. And he, too, smoked in silence for an instant. But that instant was enough to convince him what lay in Peta's mind. She had a conventional streak. That touch of prudishness which had amused and charmed him in Calcutta. It would be such fun to overcome it. He even allowed himself to toy with the thought of marrying Peta. She was enchantingly pretty and just the sort of girl the 'old folks' at home would like. Auburn, himself the most modern of moderns, came of old-fashioned parents who hated the smart society circle in which Auburn usually moved. And although they never interfered with him, he knew that they hated his various 'affairs.' At any rate he had never had the experience of being engaged to anybody. Supposing he embarked upon an engagement with this girl? It might be interesting and if she ceased to make his heart beat at this abnormal rate, well, he could always break with her. Suddenly he said:

'We're going to be married one day, though, aren't we?'

Peta looked at him speechlessly. And when at length she was able to speak she could not really show him how immeasurably those few words, spoken so casually by him, thrilled her, changed the face of the world for her. She could only say:

'Are we?'

'Why not?'

'I didn't think . . . oh, I don't know what I thought. I'm just quite incapable of thinking at all.'

'Me too,' he said lazily, 'so don't let's either of us think. Let's just consider ourselves engaged to be married. And now what about that plane?'

Peta thought it high time she told him about Noel. But she also made up her mind, there and then, that she would not tell Auburn everything. He had asked her to marry him. Ah, hadn't she known that he was serious? Hadn't she told Noel, on the boat, resented it when he suggested otherwise? How heavenly it was! Auburn loved her, and she was going to marry him, and that other marriage wouldn't count. She must tell Auburn eventually. But first she must get her freedom. She felt that she was justified in saying nothing about the marriage just now. Why should she risk losing the man she loved just because she had been kind and compassionate to another man?

She told Auburn about her meeting and friendship with Dr. Frensham on board, and why she had disembarked with him the day before yesterday.

When she had finished, Auburn said:

'But, my darling child, it was a crazy thing to do. I suppose you were sorry for the chap and all that, but he asked a hell of a lot of you.'

She felt that she must defend Noel.

'Don't blame him, Burn. He was much too ill to realise what he really was doing, and I hadn't the heart to refuse. He seemed so bent on my going ashore with him.'

'H'm. Well, I think it was pretty drastic. However, it's turned out well because we've met, which we wouldn't have done otherwise.'

'Yes, there's that way of looking at it.'

'Harley Street surgeon, is he?'

'No, a physician—heart specialist. His

75

consulting-room is in Wimpole Street.'

'Comes to the same thing. Bit of a quack, do you think?'

'No, I think he's a very good man. They all think so at the hospital. He has a reputation.'

'Young or old?'

'A little older than you are, I imagine.'

'I'm nearly thirty.'

'Oh, he's thirty-nine or so.'

'You seem to know a lot about him,' said Auburn with a touch of jealousy. 'Is he an attractive fellow?'

She admitted that she had found Noel an interesting companion and that she liked him. Auburn threw away his cigarette and pulled her back into his arms.

'I'm damned if I'm going to have you interested in this doctor. You belong to me, do you hear?'

She thrilled to those words and clung close to him.

'I know I do. I know that, darling Burn.'

He began to kiss her passionately again, and there was no clear thought left in Peta's head except that she dared not tell him that she had married Noel. She had not thought it possible to feel as intensely as this about any man. It was a kind of delirium, an enchantment from which she might pray never to be released, for it was so sweet.

Holding her close, Auburn said:

'Swear you don't care about that fellow.'

76

'But of course I don't. He's just a friend—an acquaintance. He was terribly ill and I nursed him. That's all.'

'If you had nursed me I'd have broken all records for temperatures and I'd certainly have fallen in love with you. Is this man in love with you?'

'No, no, not a bit. It isn't like that. If I could only explain . . .'

'You have explained, Sweetness, and I quite understand,' he said. 'I'm only teasing you. I adore you and I'm jealous of your doctor fellow. But you've done enough for him. Now you must come back to England with me.'

'I can't do that, Burn.'

'Why not?'

'Because Dr. Frensham is still very ill and I promised to stay a day or two longer.'

She blurted out the words desperately. She felt mean and underhand, keeping the whole truth from Auburn, yet she felt that she owed it to herself. But she must get things cleared up before she left Noel, and she knew that it was impossible for her to make that flight with her lover, much as she wanted to do so.

She remained adamant on that score, despite Auburn's arguments and pleadings. She must, she said, remain in Port Said a few days longer.

Auburn was annoyed. He was used to getting his own way. This was what made Peta different from the other women, who said 'yes' so easily. And in spite of his annoyance he was intrigued by the opposition.

'Oh, well,' he grumbled, 'if you feel it's necessary . . . but I should have thought you'd done enough for the fellow.'

Peta avoided Auburn's gaze.

'He's still dreadfully weak and ill.'

'If he wasn't I wouldn't let you stay. You're too beautiful. Will you promise to take the next boat?'

It made her feel warm and happy to think that she mattered so much to Auburn. She was confident now that he was as much in love with her as she was with him, incredible though it seemed. She promised to take that next boat. She told herself that everything would be settled between herself and Noel quite quickly and easily.

Auburn said:

'My people are a bit sticky to deal with. I'll see them when I get home and tell them about you, and until then let's keep our engagement to ourselves, shall we?'

That seemed to her reasonable. A trifle wistfully she said:

'You're probably expected to make a brilliant marriage, and I'm just . . .'

'You're just adorable,' he interrupted, 'and just what they'll like.' And he caught her back in his arms.

While she rested there, he told himself that he was really very much in love with this girl.

But already in his mind he was shying at that word 'engagement.' He wanted Peta and he was prepared to say or do anything in order to get her. And the fact that other men wanted her sharpened desire in him. That sick doctor in the hospital . . . possibly he was in love with her, too, although Peta wouldn't admit it.

Auburn wasn't particularly pleased about leaving her in Port Said, but he had no choice. The business which took him on to London this afternoon was urgent. He was engaged for lunch, too, which was a nuisance, but he couldn't put off the man who had come all the way from Cairo to meet him. He had to let Peta go. She went, carrying with her the impression of an Auburn wholly in love with her, carrying with her, too, that letter of confession about her marriage to Noel Frensham. It lay, still unopened, in her bag.

CHAPTER SEVEN

Peta saw little of Noel that day. He had made a sensational recovery, but he was still in need of all the attention the doctors and nurses could give him, and essentially in need of rest, of freedom from any worries.

Peta had a dozen and one things that she wanted to ask. Questions that were of burning importance to her, to put to him. So much to be talked over and arranged. But she could do none of it. She knew that she must wait until he was strong enough to stand anxiety. Sheer kindness of heart made her take trouble to make things as easy as possible for him—he seemed so pathetically remorseful for having dragged her into this marriage 'under false pretences,' as he said. But she assured him again and again that it wasn't his fault that things had gone this way, and that he must stop worrying.

In consequence Noel slept a great deal, so Peta saw no necessity to remain glued to his side as she had been while his condition was critical. She wanted to see Auburn again. He was not leaving Port Said until late afternoon and they arranged another hour or two together at his hotel. They spent those hectic hours seated under an awning in a palm court which had a cool fountain in it, spraying silver drops of water over the loveliest flowers, while a South American dance band played the latest airs from England and America.

An Egyptian servant in a white uniform wearing a red fez served them with tea. Peta could eat none of the delicious looking sandwiches or iced cakes, but drank her tea thirstily and Auburn ignored the tea altogether and sipped gin and lime juice.

'I wish to heaven I could see you somewhere by yourself. The whole darn place is full of people at this hour,' Auburn grumbled.

And Peta said a little wildly:

'And I wish to heaven that you weren't leaving me behind.'

'You know what I think about that,' he said. 'But you will stay and minister to your doctor friend.'

She kept silent. Rather miserably she asked herself why she did not make a full confession to Auburn, but she found herself no more able to do so now than this morning.

Her gaze kept wandering to her wrist watch. Auburn would be leaving so soon. The time was rushing by, and it was just more than she could bear, saying good-bye to him. He had been dear to her before, but now he was a thousand times dearer because he had told her that he loved her, and she was going to marry him.

Auburn left her in no doubt that he was in love with her. Every look, every gesture, every word was perfect from her point of view. He was a born lover. He noticed everything about her and told her so. Noticed, for instance, that she had put little pearl stud earrings in her ears which had not been there this morning, and said that he liked them and that they made her look *chic*. He liked that flowered green and white *crêpe de Chine* dress, with the little green silk cape, into which she had changed from the grey flannel suit, and was duly impressed when she told him that she had made it herself. With delightful familiarity he

81

leaned towards her and pulled her white straw hat with its green ribbon at a more rakish angle over her eye, and said:

'You look rather wicked like that, baby heart.'

Peta, enraptured, could only flush rosily and laugh for sheer happiness.

'You're such a darling, Burn,' she said. 'But why want me to look wicked!'

He stretched his long legs before him and smiled at her through his long lashes.

'I'm just fooling. You couldn't look anything but good. You've got the eyes of an angel and I want to take you in my arms and never let you go again.'

'Oh Burn, how many girls have you said things like that to?'

'None,' he said, and his blue bad eyes wandered over her head and were held a moment by an extremely pretty woman who had just entered the palm court with two men.

But Peta looked at Auburn—wondered if any other man with such long limbs, moved so gracefully, or if, indeed, there was another man in the world to touch Auburn Lyell. She was not so silly as to believe that she was really the only girl to whom he had said lovely things. But she wanted to believe that he loved her more than he had loved anybody else, and that was all that mattered.

'I can pick up another boat the day after tomorrow,' she said, 'so in about ten days' time

I shall see you again.'

'You must cable me every day,' he said.

Peta shook her head at him.

'Darling, I'm not a millionaire. Are you always so extravagant?'

'Always,' he said, 'and hope I always shall be. Economy is so dull. And you shall be extravagant, too, when you're mine, darling. You're much too adorable to earn twenty-five bob a week looking after the Bradleys' horrid little boy, and have to make your own clothes and count the pennies. You ought to do nothing but sit about looking glorious in the most divine clothes, give cocktail parties and go to them, dance, do shows, drive a Rolls Bentley down to the South of France and play roulette and—'

'Don't go on, darling, because you're bewildering me!' Peta broke in, laying a protesting hand on his knee.

'Oh, I could continue that list *ad infinitum.*'

'You rather take my breath away, darling.'

He let his gaze rest on her upper lip and said irrelevantly:

'That upper lip of yours would drive any man mad.'

Peta shook her head at him speechlessly. He did indeed take her breath away. He would just storm the citadel of any woman's heart. He was so gay and absurd and serious, too. All the things combined.

Now and then a faint doubt rose in her

mind as to whether she could ever be what he wished, do all that he wanted her to do. She wasn't really the sort of girl who drove about the South of France in expensive cars and haunted cocktail parties and did nothing but 'sit round and look lovely.'

There was a very genuine domestic streak in Peta. One could, she supposed, be domestic without being dull, although the reverse idea seemed to lie in the minds of people who presented the Dietrichs and the Garbos and the Joan Crawfords to a jazz-mad, sensation-loving world. Perhaps warming the slipper at the hearthside was looked at askance. Well, Peta had no more desire than any other woman to be so steeped in domesticity that she couldn't enjoy herself, and she thought it was the most exciting thing in the world to visualise herself rushing round the South of France with a man like Auburn Lyell at her side. But would he be bored with her in time?

She found herself asking the question aloud.

'Are you sure I'm exciting enough for you, Burn?'

He, filled with the intoxication of her youth and her physical charm, laughed and nodded:

'You bet your sweet life.'

She could only look at him mistily, and tell herself that she was the luckiest girl alive.

'How is the sick doctor, by the way?' Auburn asked casually.

That made Peta draw in her breath and look

away from Auburn. She felt so guilty. Inside this very bag which she was holding lay the wedding-ring which Noel Frensham had put on her finger and which she had had no scruples in removing before she came out to meet Auburn. She said:

'A bit better, but still terribly weak.'

'Well, weak or not weak, you're to take the next boat to England and wire me at my Club the moment you arrive.'

'I promise.'

'Where will you go?'

'Straight to the Bradleys.'

'They'll be at their London house, I suppose . . .' Auburn pulled a diary out of his pocket and flicked over one or two pages . . . 'I've got their address somewhere.'

'Avenue road, St. John's Wood.'

'Ah, yes, that's it. They've got one of these dull, highly respectable houses with a nice tennis court, a conservatory and all the comforts.'

Peta did not answer. There were times when Auburn perplexed her. He said such confusing things. He was always deriding respectability, for instance, which she did not quite understand because she, herself, did not feel at all like that. Perhaps it was because she had been brought up in what Auburn would call a 'dull and highly respectable house.' And to her the Bradleys' home had seemed rather a fine one. She had had a beautifully furnished bedroom and Derek's schoolroom was quite modern and charming.

Auburn called for another gin and lime with plenty of ice in it. He murmured:

'I'll get in touch with you there, my sweet.'

She nodded. There were so many things she wanted to say, to ask about their future together. Did he intend to take her straight to his people and introduce her as his future wife? Did he want her to leave her job and marry him soon? Oh, lots of things. But in her present position, she did not feel she ought to ask him such questions. First she must get her freedom. It was just as well that Auburn did not insist on an immediate open engagement. She said:

'Do you suppose the Bradleys will be so furious with me for staying on here that they won't let me go back to them?'

'Dunno,' said Auburn, yawning. 'But I'll fix Mary Bradley. She's always had rather a passion for me.'

Peta shook her head at him.

'You're dreadfully vain, darling.'

'Dreadfully in love with you,' he parried, and caught her hand and kissed it.

And after that the time seemed to rush by and Peta found herself saying good-bye to him—driving in a car to the Aerodrome from which Auburn was to take his plane. Her heart was sinking at the sight of all his strapped, labelled luggage, and the thought that he was going to fly all those thousands of miles away from her and that there were so many difficulties ahead of her before she would really find peace and happiness again. She could only cling to him, and close her eyes while he held her tightly to his heart and his eager lips covered her face and throat with kisses.

Fired by her response, Auburn half inclined to kidnap her there and then, he said, and force her into the plane with him. But she was an obstinate little thing, he said, and he must leave her behind. And heaven help her, he said, if she didn't take the next boat and put an end for good and all to playing the Samaritan to strange sick doctors.

She wept and laughed in turns, swept off her feet by his passionate love-making, his gaiety and his whole dominant personality. With her lips still stinging from his kisses, divinely happy and desperately unhappy, she stood and watched the plane take off and disappear into the blue obscurity of distance, whilst she waved wildly with a handkerchief. Then she drove back in the car to the hospital, telling herself that she had only one desire in the world now, and that was to sever this superficial tie of marriage with poor Noel Frensham. Why poor? She had nothing to pity him for now, really. He was going to get well and he obviously would not want to remain married to her.

The ecstatic nervous trembling which had seized her limbs during the last few minutes with Auburn ceased before she reached the hospital. She managed to take the ring from her bag and put it on her finger before she went indoors. After all, she still had some sort of position to keep up in the eyes of the hospital-staff and for Dr. Frensham's sake.

That same evening she was told by doctors and the sister-in-charge that 'her husband' had made wonderful strides during the day, and since his pulse and heart were so much stronger tonight she might sit and talk to him without fear of tiring him.

Peta was greatly relieved to hear it. There was so much to be said between Noel and herself.

When she had had her supper, she went to his room and found him propped up against the pillows looking decidedly better. His colour had improved and there was a more normal look about his eyes, although in the dim light of the bed-table lamp he still looked very frail, Peta thought.

Her passion for Auburn Lyell made her feel just a little resentful towards Noel, although, of course, she knew he had influenced her into the marriage for her own sake and that she had nobody but herself to blame. She tried not to show her resentment. And the smile he gave her and the hand he held out in greeting, were so full of friendliness, that her young heart, which was fundamentally kind, softened towards him.

'I'm terribly glad you're so much stronger,' she said, and placed her fingers in his for the fraction of a second.

'I feel a new man,' he said. 'I know now that I *am* going to get well.'

'Of course.'

'I've got good recuperative powers and I mean to be up and about quite soon and get you back to England.'

Peta flushed and opened her lips as though to speak, but closed them again. Frensham, smoking the first cigarette which he had been allowed, blew the smoke through his nostrils and watched her, thinking not for the first time what remarkable features the child had . . . such lovely eyes and such a glorious colour tonight. He said gently:

'What have you been doing today?'

A trifle nervously she answered:

'Quite a lot of things. I—I've written to the Bradleys and I—' She paused, stammering.

'Tell me,' said Noel.

She decided to tell him.

'As a matter of fact I went into an hotel to ask about a room because I can't very well stay in the hospital any longer—they want the nurses' room—and I met . . . I met *him*.'

'You mean the man you're interested in?'

'Yes. He didn't fly to England straight away after all. He stopped here on business. It was an amazing coincidence.'

'H'm,' said Noel. 'And he must have been amazed to find you here.'

'He was.'

Noel's gaze did not leave her. He could see how the colour in her cheeks changed to a deeper carmine and how her breath quickened, and he felt a peculiar pang of jealousy that this unknown man should be capable of rousing her so. She was Mrs. Noel Frensham! Well that, of course, was laughable. And she wouldn't be his wife much longer. But he felt an overpowering curiosity about the man with whom Peta was so obviously in love.

'Tell me everything, Peta,' he said. 'This man—did you let him know about—us?'

'No. I—I saw no reason why I should because I—hoped—it would be all settled up quickly and quietly and that it would be better to tell him when it was over, otherwise he might think all sorts of things that weren't true.'

'You mean he might imagine that you had had an "affair" with me?'

She gave a confused little laugh.

'He might.'

Noel's lips curved into a faint, ironic smile.

'Oh, well, we must convince him that there's nothing of that sort. But what does this man actually mean to you, Peta? You're in love with him. I can see that. Is he in love with you?'

Her dark curly head went back proudly.

'Yes.'

'You weren't so sure of that when you first told me about him on the boat.'

'I'm sure now.'

'Has he asked you to marry him?'

'Yes.'

'And you—accepted?'

She swallowed nervously and her fingers twitched about the little chiffon handkerchief which she held.

'There was no question of an—an engagement. He wants to see what his parents feel about things. We're going to become engaged when I get back.'

'Why should it matter what his parents think? Is he under age?'

Peta was forced to giggle.

'Good heavens, no! He's very much a man and has control of one of the biggest businesses in India.'

Frensham's deep eyes questioned her silently for an instant. His brows went up.

'I don't quite understand that. If he's a man of means and able to do what he wants, shouldn't he be able to get engaged if he wants?'

Peta felt that Noel was trying to be derogatory about Auburn, and, whether he was justified or not, she was angry in a purely feminine, illogical fashion.

'Whatever Burn does, I am sure is for the best,' she exclaimed.

Frensham smiled broadly at that. Dear little pompous thing, he thought. So sweetly defending her lover, and quite rightly. But why was the man hedging about the engagement? He had hedged in Calcutta. Noel didn't like it. He was perfectly well aware that anybody as young and inexperienced and soft as Peta would be easy prey to an attractive man whose intentions were not quite honourable, and who was subtle enough to keep her guessing.

'Don't be cross with me for making suggestions, my dear,' he said. 'Naturally I'm interested in you—and this man.'

'Oh, I know. And you're very kind—you always have been.'

On an impulse Noel said:

'I suppose you won't consider staying as you are—married to me?'

She started and flushed scarlet.

'Oh, no,' she said in a frightened voice.

That note of fear distressed him more than he would have cared to admit even to himself. But he had become strangely fond of Peta. He wished there was no 'other man.' Had she been quite fancy-free, alone in the world as he was, she might not have minded remaining his wife. But, of course, if she was in love with this fellow, he could understand her reluctance, even her momentary fear at the mere idea. He said:

'That's all right, Peta. You needn't remain my wife.'

'You wouldn't want me to, would you?' she asked, feeling embarrassed.

He wasn't quite prepared to answer that, so he said irrelevantly:

'I've got a disappointment in store for you, Peta. It's been a bit of a shock to me, but this annulment business isn't going to be quite as simple as I hoped.'

Her heart knocked.

'Oh, why?'

'Well, I had a lawyer fellow to see me this afternoon while you were out—an English chap who works out here and whom Dr. Lane recommended. We discussed the business because I thought I ought to know about it and be able to tell you what to expect, as quickly as possible.'

'What did he say?'

Frensham told her, realising as he did so that she would be upset. He had not been too happy about it himself. Marriages were not easily annulled. The case would have to be tried in England. It would be impossible to keep it altogether private, and the details which would have to be given to the judge in order to prove justification for annulment, would be embarrassing beyond description— so much so that Frensham was certain that Peta would never go through with it. He did not think it necessary to give her those details, but he said enough to make her cheeks scorch, and for her to shrink at the mere thought of having to get into a witness-box and answer the questions that would be put to her.

While Noel was still speaking, letting her down as gently as he could, she interrupted with a cry:

'Oh, it would be impossible! *Impossible!'*

Frensham nodded.

'I felt that myself. I'm afraid one rushes into these things without thinking. Indeed, as you know, I never for a moment imagined I was going to live. Like anybody else who knows nothing of the law, I imagined annulment to be simple, and I have been informed that it is far more difficult than common-or-garden divorce.'

Peta's heart sank like a stone in her breast. Her flaming cheeks grew pale. She had a swift, awful vision of losing Auburn—her adorable lover—almost as soon as she had found him.

'Oh, what can we do?' she exclaimed. 'What on earth can we do now? I knew something like this would happen. I *knew.'*

Frensham put out a hand to her.

'Don't upset yourself, child. We'll do something. I'm not going to let you down. I dragged you into this and I'll get you out of it.'

There were tears in her eyes and real distress in her heart which he could see and which caused him an even greater distress. Somehow he hated to think that she so hated her position as his wife. He stroked her hand gently, as a brother would have done.

'Poor little Peta. Don't look so wild, my dear. There's such a thing as divorce, you know.'

'You mean—?'

'I mean that since annulment is so darned difficult and unpleasant for all concerned, we must arrange a divorce. *That* won't be pleasant, but it will be more so than the other.'

The colour returned to her cheeks.

'Oh, Dr. Frensham—I mean Noel—how will we get it?'

He scratched his cheek reflectively and the faintest glint of humour came into his sunken eyes.

'There are lots of ways, my dear. I can be unfaithful to you or you can be unfaithful to me.'

She was panic-stricken again.

'But we can't—we mustn't have too much publicity.'

He grew serious once more.

'My dear child, I'm dreadfully sorry for having involved you in this show, but it just won't be possible to make it altogether private. Unfortunately I'm too darned well-known in my profession. Obviously I shall have to furnish you with details of a faked affair and you will sue me for divorce, and the newspapers will get hold of it. I can't stop it. I wish I could.'

She put both hands to her cheeks.

'Then everyone will think—Burn will think—that I—that I've been your *wife*. That

95

isn't fair—oh, it isn't fair!'

'I'm sorry, Peta,' he repeated, 'and I know it isn't fair. But we're rather between the devil and the deep sea. I think it would be worse for you to try to get an annulment.'

'It'll be bad anyhow,' she said chokingly.

'This man—if he loves you—will surely believe what you tell him. And you can tell him the whole story, and so will I.'

'Yes, I suppose he will.'

'He wouldn't be worth loving if he didn't, Peta. He already knows that you put off at Port Said to see a dying man through and that there was never any question of love between us. Of course he'll believe you.'

For a moment Peta sat silent, feeling and looking rather desperate. Now that it was all over, it seemed so appallingly evident that she had been mad to marry Noel Frensham. She might have known that such things are more easily done than undone. The difficulties were increasing and the shadow between Auburn and herself seemed to be growing larger and blacker and more formidable every second. The quiet annulment for which she had hoped was out of the question. It would mean all those horrifying, intimate details at which Noel had hinted. Examinations and humiliations on both sides. No—divorce was the only way out. And that, too, must be public. She heard Noel's voice—still weak from his illness and a trifle ironic:

96

'It isn't turning out too badly for you, really, my dear. You'll be able to claim a third of my income, and that's considerable. And I won't begrudge it to you, either.'

'I wouldn't dream of taking it!' she said, shocked.

He sighed.

'Do you dislike me so much? Do you feel so unfriendly? You were so grand to me while I was ill. I don't like to feel you've turned against me because of this.'

She stopped thinking of herself and turned her thoughts to Noel. She was being rather mean and selfish, she told herself, concentrating on her own affairs in this way. After all, Noel had married her in the first place in order to benefit her, and here she was being horrid, making him feel that he ought to have died. It was really rotten of her. Filled with remorse, she put out a hand and gripped his thin fingers.

'I don't dislike you at all, Noel. You know that. And I don't feel in the least unfriendly. Naturally it's all a bit of a shock—this business about getting my freedom.'

'I understand.'

'And of course it isn't any easier for you,' she added.

'No, I can't say I want to be mixed up in a divorce case and turned into an unfaithful husband when I haven't been a husband at all!' he said dryly.

'There's your reputation as a doctor! It'll be rotten for you. Oh, the whole thing's rotten!'

'Well, it must be faced. I made the mistake of living when I should have died.'

'But that's what you mustn't feel!' she said. 'Honestly you mustn't. It's marvellous to think that you're going to live.'

He knew that she was being sincere. He knew, also, that there wasn't a grain of malice in Peta. She was just a natural, impulsive child. And he was so fond of her. Too fond. He thought much too much about her while he had been lying here through the long lonely hours on his bed of sickness. He had even dreamed of her taking her place at his side as his wife, bringing her sweetness, her loveliness to him to round off his existence. A trifle sadly he said:

'If there hadn't been this other man I think I would have asked you to stay with me, Peta.'

Her lashes flickered nervously and she did not look at him. It was the second time he had hinted that he would have liked her to remain his wife. She wondered how she would have felt about it if there had been no Auburn—if she had met Noel Frensham on the boat going out to India, instead of coming back. He was a clever doctor and a charming person. She might have been very thrilled with him under different circumstances. But she couldn't imagine being thrilled by him now. Now that she was held in a mental and physical thrall by

98

Auburn Lyell.

After a pause, she said:

'The only thing for me to do will be to tell Burn when I get back to England, and trust to God that he will believe in me.'

'Of course he will. The next thing for me to do is to furnish you with the evidence for the divorce.'

She felt distressed for him.

'You'll loathe that.'

'I will. But if you want to be free to marry this fellow, there's no other course for me to take.'

'I think it's rather grand of you,' she said.

He felt a sudden unreasonable dislike of the 'other man' welling up in him. He might have stood a chance with Peta if it hadn't been for this fellow. God knew he recoiled from the very thought of faked evidence for a divorce and of having to let his friends and acquaintances—and patients—imagine that he had made a ridiculous marriage during his holiday, and barely stuck to it more than a few weeks. A rotten, regrettable business. The annulment would have been better from his point of view, but not from Peta's, and he wasn't going to put her through the humiliation of *that*. After all, she had only married him out of sheer kindness of her young heart.

Then he said, suddenly:

'What's this fellow's name, Peta?'

She answered:

'Auburn Lyell. He's the son of Bernard Lyell, who owns, I believe, tremendous business houses in India and England.' She saw Noel Frensham start involuntarily and a slight colour come on his hollowed cheeks.

'Auburn Lyell!' he repeated, and said again: '*Auburn Lyell!*'

'Yes. Do you know him?'

Frensham made no reply. He had broken into a cold sweat from head to foot. His heart, weakened by the terrible fevers, was pounding, pounding. He tried to speak. A mist came between Peta's charming face and his vision. He gasped:

'A nurse . . . please . . .'

And then, from sheer weakness, he fainted.

Peta, having not the least idea why her lover's name should have had such an effect upon Noel, jumped to her feet and rushed for a nurse. The fainting fit was a brief one and Frensham was speedily revived, but he refused to continue his discussion with Peta. He bade her a somewhat brief good night and asked to be left alone. The nurse encouraged him to lie quiet, so Peta went to her room in a state of anxiety and indecision, remembering a dozen questions that she had meant to ask Noel, and pursued by a dozen fresh doubts and worries which, the longer she thought about the whole situation, increased.

Why had Noel fainted like that? What did he know about Auburn? Or was it just her imagination that the name had had any effect upon him? Sister said that she thought it was just that he had talked too much. He was still far from strong.

Sleep did not come easily to Peta that night, but when she did eventually close her eyes, it was the memory of Auburn rather than of Noel that haunted her. She thought of him as she had seen him just before he boarded the plane, gay, handsome, smiling, waving farewell to her. Her whole being was filled with ecstasy then. She knew that he loved her and that he must, he *would* believe in her and help her out of this tangle. Nothing else mattered to her. Nothing else could matter so much in her life again.

CHAPTER EIGHT

The doctors had drugged Noel Frensham to sleep, but he awoke in the early hours of the morning, and feeling rather sick and unhappy, lay still, watching the sudden flushing of the dawn-light through his window, and listening to the faint cries and sounds that came from a distance, heralding the fact that Port Said was awake.

Frensham was haunted by memories of the past, and by one spectre in particular. The pale ghost of a girl who had been a patient of his,

101

and who had died in his West End Nursing Home about two years ago. She had been nothing to him but an interesting case, and as such he had remembered her. But, like many of his patients, she had confided in him and he was possibly one of the only people in the world who knew the real cause of her death.

Toni Maitland, her name had been. A film actress. Not a very successful one, because she couldn't act, but she had had a ravishing little face and was blonde and petite, and directors found that she photographed well, so she made her living out of 'walk-ons' and small parts. She was barely twenty-one when she was taken by ambulance from the flat which she shared in a Mayfair mews with another girl into the Nursing Home to which Frensham sent most of his patients. And it was there that Frensham had learned that she had tried to commit suicide and had only just been prevented from ending her life by the friend who had found her in time. But she did not come under Noel's control soon enough. Her heart was seriously affected and nothing he could do prevented the thread of her young life from snapping. Such a frail thread it had been and she had seemed so anxious to end everything.

One evening he was called in to her and sat beside her bed wondering why a child so lovely, so naturally gay, pleasure-loving and flimsy-minded, should want to get out of a life from which she seemed to have extracted the maximum of pleasure.

Then with great sorrowful eyes fixed on him and in between great, panting breaths, while her poor little heart beat out its last pathetic broken rhythm, Toni Maitland told Frensham about—Auburn Lyell.

She had met Lyell at a studio party given by a film director and into which she and her girl friend, she said, had managed to 'gate-crash.' Auburn Lyell was there—the most handsome and the most attractive man she had ever met, and she had met a few, she said. He had made wild love to her immediately. He liked little, big-eyed, baby-faced women, especially when they had a certain amount of reserve, and Toni had never been one to make herself cheap. She had led a Bohemian life, but she wasn't prepared to throw herself into the arms of any man, no matter how much he attracted her. She had old-fashioned ideas about love and she wanted to get married and be through with the film studio business. But Auburn Lyell had been too much for her. There was something about him, she had told Frensham, that a woman couldn't resist, and she had fallen for him—badly—in every sense of the word. He had promised to marry her, but asked that their engagement should be a secret one, because his father had other views and he wanted to break the news to his parents gradually.

Lying here in his narrow hospital bed, Frensham recalled every word that Toni Maitland had told him. With almost horrifying clarity they stood out in his memory and it seemed that that explanation for the secret engagement was the very one that Peta had given, last night. These secret engagements seemed to be Auburn Lyell's hobby.

Of course he had never had the slightest intention of marrying Toni Maitland, and when he got tired of her he told her so.

But the thing had gone too far in Toni's life and she had tried to kill herself. And that time she had been saved, because her friend had sent for Lyell and he had stopped it by giving her fresh hope—anxious, of course, that there should not be an inquest and any mud slung at him.

For another three months he had held her on the end of a string, jogging her like a puppet, whichever way he willed. Then some married woman had captivated his fancy and for the second time he left Toni cold. After that—another period of despair for her. She had begun to lose her looks. She had grown too thin and angular for the camera and could get no work. She was hard up, and she was sick in body and mind, still pitifully enslaved by the man who had seduced and broken her. Then had followed the second attempt at suicide and after that the heart-attack which had brought her under Frensham's notice.

When he had asked how she had been able to afford to enter his Home, she had told him that Lyell had sent her friend the money. Lyell had gone out East and rid himself of responsibility. But before he went, the friend had told him that Toni was dying, so he had salved what little conscience he possessed by making death easy for her, knowing that he had made life intolerable.

It was by no means an uncommon story and one that Noel Frensham had heard before, but somehow it had shocked him and remained in his memory, and when poor little Toni Maitland died he was beside her, and her last words had been:

'Tell Auburn . . . I . . . loved him so!'

Those words, so generous and so pitiful, had roused Noel to a state of fury against the man concerned. But of course it had been no business of his, and there was nothing he could do or wished to do. But he did see Toni's friend and he heard enough from her that under the good looks and the attractiveness, young Lyell was a heartless cur. He remembered it up against him. And long after Toni Maitland had been laid in her grave, Frensham, always about town meeting all kinds of people, heard young Lyell's name, and from time to time made casual inquiries, and found always the same answer. Auburn Lyell was a rotter with women. Rotten through and through. He had never played fair—never been known to—but at the same time he conducted his little games cautiously so that he kept himself out of trouble, and came between husbands and wives without allowing himself to be turned into a co-respondent. Wherever he went he left a trail of havoc, and still women fell for him. No matter what they heard, they fell, believing that they would be the ones whom he would really love! Such was feminine vanity.

Noel Frensham had often wondered if the day would arrive when he would come face to face with the man who had morally murdered Toni Maitland, and probably a few others besides, if facts were known. But he had not thought it would come to pass in a way that would affect him personally.

And here it was! Auburn Lyell was the man who had met Peta out in Calcutta and captivated her—as he had done the rest. Peta was only another butterfly, circling round the candle flame, confident that her own wings would never be scorched. And to Peta he had given that same absurd explanation why the engagement must be a secret one. Because of his parents

Secret, yes, because Auburn Lyell had not the slightest intention of getting married. He had too good a time as a bachelor. And even if he did marry, God help his wife, thought Frensham.

Hour after hour, Noel brooded over the

106

affair, writhing at the thought that such a man held Peta in the hollow of his hand. Peta, who was, in her fashion, little and sweet and soft, like Toni Maitland had been. Only Toni had had a flimsy, silly little mind, and Peta was intelligent and fine and a hundred times more idealistic. It appalled Frensham to think of Peta's reactions should a man like Lyell get complete possession of her, mind and body, then throw her over as he had done the others.

Peta, who had been his little friend and good angel! Peta, whom he had made his wife and to whom he had meant to leave all his worldly goods. *She* was to be numbered amongst the conquests of a man who, so far as women were concerned, had a vile reputation wheresoever he went, East or West.

Frensham knew perfectly well, now, that a man had only to enter a Club in London or Calcutta, and he would hear of young Lyell's latest unsavoury 'affair' out of which he had managed to wriggle unscathed, leaving disaster behind him.

No, it was unthinkable to Noel that such a man should be allowed to ruin Peta's life. It was time someone showed the fellow up. And Noel decided there and then that he must at all costs make Peta see the folly of loving, of believing in such a man.

At the same time Noel Frensham was too astute, too clever a psychologist to make the mistake of attacking Auburn openly now, whilst he, Noel, and Peta were still in Port Said. No matter what he had to say about Auburn, Peta would be loyal—yes, Noel knew that loyalty was an integral part of Peta's nature. She would refuse to hear ill against her lover, or if she listened she would repudiate it—follow in the footsteps of other women who had loved Auburn, and go blindly on, believing that she alone could reform him.

Futile to beg Peta now, this moment, to give up her hopes of marriage with Auburn Lyell. Better to wait until they returned to London, where he could, perhaps, gather some conclusive proofs about the man's character and furnish her with them.

And supposing she did not mind? Supposing Auburn could convince her that he meant to marry her? Supposing even that he *did* marry her and that he had, at last, found a girl to whom he could be faithful? That made the thing little better in Noel Frensham's mind. He would loathe to think of that girl going to the embrace of such a man. And suddenly it came upon Noel Frensham that his desire to save Peta from Auburn Lyell was not altogether impersonal. He loved the child. Loved her for her straight, generous nature, her sweetness, her kindness of heart. In order to go to a decent man who would make her happy, he would have been pleased to set her free. If not pleased, at least resigned. But he would not willingly allow her to go to Auburn

Lyell. No, my God, rather than do that, he would repudiate his word and make no effort to give her a divorce.

The longer he thought about it, the stronger grew Noel's feelings towards Peta and a certain fierce pleasure in the knowledge that she was his wife—that he had legal claim to her if none other—and that he could make it extremely difficult for her to get her freedom.

Auburn Lyell would never take her away, would not make himself a co-respondent or put himself out in any way. Frensham knew that. He felt he would be safe in assuming that Auburn would expect *her* to get the divorce.

Then he reproached himself for carrying the thing too far in his mind. There might be no necessity to force Peta to act, one way or the other. Perhaps she would be sensible and throw up all her ambitions about Auburn, once she knew what he really was. But any 'showing up' that was to be done, must be achieved in London.

He could temporise by suggesting that she must be very careful what she did if she wanted this divorce to go through. He would also suggest that she should, for the time being, live, to all intents and purposes, as his wife.

In that way he could protect her. He *must*. With his newfound feeling surging up in Frensham, there was not a particle of his being that did not recoil at the idea of letting Peta share Toni Maitland's fate.

And he thought:

'There must be a special hell reserved for men like Lyell, who take the very young and break them for a moment's pleasure!'

His very emotions bred in Frensham a stronger desire than ever to get strong and well quickly. So that he could protect *her*, his little friend of the voyage, his wife.

'*To have and to hold—until death us do part,*' he had said when they were being married, and when he had thought he was dying. Well, now that he was to live he felt he would rather that death, than a man like Auburn Lyell, should part him from Peta.

Nothing of the mental storm that had shaken him at dawn was apparent to Peta when she visited him later that morning. He seemed calm, and full of a quiet determination to rise from his sick-bed and take the first possible boat back to England. Almost Peta's first question was about Auburn Lyell, and what Noel knew; what had caused him to faint the previous night? But Frensham merely gave her a baffling smile and replied in non-committal fashion.

He knew Lyell, he said—not personally, but by repute. Just what he knew, he did not tell, and why he had fainted he did not explain. He said that since Peta's ambition was to return to England without further delay, she had better do so. But on certain conditions. That she travelled as Mrs. Frensham, and as Mrs. Frensham went straight to his home in London and took up her residence there as his wife.

'My housekeeper, Mrs. McLeod, who runs my house and is a very able woman, will be informed of your coming. I will send her a letter by airmail today and she will make you comfortable,' Noel said. 'And as soon as I am fit enough to travel, I'll come back and we'll settle the future.'

This proposal caused Peta great agitation.

'I would so much rather not do that,' she said. 'I don't want to—to have to take my place as your wife.'

'My dear child, there will be no wifely duties expected of you other than that of using my name and my home,' he said dryly. 'But if you want to sue me for divorce you'll have at least to let the Court assume that you have lived as my wife.'

Peta took a cigarette out of the box beside his bed and lit it. Her fingers trembled. He could see that she was in a bad state of nerves. He added gently:

'I know you're hating me and hating this whole position, but I may be doing you a good turn in the long run.'

'I don't know in what way!' she flashed.

'You *are* hating me,' he smiled, but his fine keen eyes looked uncommonly sad.

At once she held out a hand.

'No, I'm not really, Noel. But it's all very

111

awkward, and it means that I'll have to tell Burn, and you don't know what it will be to me if he doesn't believe my story.'

Frensham drew his fingers away from hers. The clasp of those small warm fingers affected him more than he would admit. Indeed, he had an unaccountable longing, this morning, to take her in his arms and kiss her, to tell her that she was a mad, misguided babe to pin her faith and her hopes upon such a cur as Lyell and to beg her to remain with him, Noel. For with him, even if she, on her side, could not feel passionate love, she would have security, peace, friendship. And she could so easily have him at her feet. He wondered grimly what she would say if he told her that he was fast falling in love with her? He, Frensham, who had been a confirmed bachelor all his life, and whom no other woman had ever moved to more than a passing emotion?

He began to argue with her gently but firmly that she must make some show of it as his wife before she could become the respondent in their divorce case. He spoke of Auburn as impersonally as he could.

'If the man is really in love with you, Peta, he'll believe you, and he'll wait until you are free.'

'I suppose I have no other choice,' she said unhappily.

'There'll be nobody to bully you—you'll just be mistress of my place, my dear,' he said with a faint smile, 'and you'll have money to burn, and once I get back you'll be able to start a nice rumour about my coldness and neglect, and then we'll see what happens.'

She realised that he was being very generous and that if he had been less honourable he might have acted in reverse fashion. She was grateful and told him so.

'I know it'll all be hateful for you,' she said. 'I feel rather mean. Because I've got so much to look forward to.'

Frensham's eyes narrowed.

'Meaning your life with Lyell?'

She nodded and a warm pink stole into her cheeks and a rapt look into her eyes which made Frensham feel sick at heart—full of an impotent rage against the man who was responsible for bringing such colour to that frank young face and such a light into those soft, believing eyes.

'Well, for the time being, be good and do as I ask, Peta,' he said abruptly. 'And remember that you must be extremely circumspect if you should meet this man before I get back, because in order to win your case against me, there must be nothing against you.'

That all sounded hateful and involved, but she knew that he was right and she gave way. Her discussion with Noel ended in him insisting upon her taking some money from him in order to settle what bills she found necessary to run up in Port Said, and for her voyage home.

Later, when she left the hospital and walked down to the P. & O. offices to see about her bookings, she knew that she ought to be relieved and light-hearted at the thought that she would soon be in London with Auburn again. But she could feel nothing but apprehension. A most awkward and unpleasant period lay in store for her. It wouldn't even be a thrill under these circumstances, acting a part as the wife of one of London's most eminent physicians and, instead of being a nursery-governess in the Bradley household, finding herself mistress of a luxurious house in Wimpole Street. And being, into the bargain, a claimant upon a third of her 'husband's' considerable income.

'Of course I won't claim the money,' she told herself. 'Auburn wouldn't want me to.'

But what would Auburn say to the whole affair? Supposing he would refuse to believe that she had never been, in fact, Dr. Frensham's wife? But of course he would, he *must* believe, otherwise the light of her life would go right out.

If only that quiet annulment had been possible! All this publicity of divorce was the last thing she had anticipated or wanted. She had done a rash thing in marrying Noel, and she was certainly going to pay for her folly, she told herself.

But she decided that she would do as Noel

114

asked, go to his home and stay there until he could join her. Whilst there she could see Auburn, and the Bradleys, and write to Aunt Annie and explain the whole crazy situation to her. How unfortunate it all had been . . . for poor Noel Frensham as well! It wasn't going to do his reputation as a medical man much good.

At the P. & O. offices she found that she could get a berth on a boat which was due at Port Said tomorrow. So she booked it for 'Mrs. Frensham.' That seemed so fantastic and unreal to her! She went back to the hospital to tell Noel that in less than twenty-four hours she would be gone. And in a little under a fortnight she would be back in England again.

When the time came for her to say good-bye to Noel, some of the real feeling of friendship and admiration which she had had for him when they had first met on board returned. She was more charming than she had been since their fatal 'deathbed marriage,' which had had the effect of making her strange and awkward with him.

Just before the car came to take her down to the boat, she sat beside Noel trying to thank him for the good things he had meant to do for her—for giving her her release at so much cost to himself—and for all his sympathy and understanding.

'You've been grand to me, and you know I don't blame you in the least for what's

115

happened,' she said.

'That's generous of you, my dear,' he said.

He needed the generosity, he thought. He felt absurdly wretched at parting from her. He knew he was going to feel very much alone when she had gone and more lonely still in the future. Heaven only knew what was going to happen in the future! But he did know that somehow he was going to prevent her from breaking her heart and ruining her life for Auburn Lyell. He liked to think that she did not blame him too much and that today, at least, they were parting as friends. He would have liked so much to tell her what really lay in his mind and heart, but dared not. And he wondered if she would loathe him should things turn out so that, for her own sake, he refused her the freedom on which she was counting.

'I shall feel horribly embarrassed, turning up at your house as your wife,' she told him.

'You needn't. They'll all like you, Peta. And I only wish it wasn't such a transitory affair, and that you didn't want to divorce me!'

Under the small brim of the little blue straw hat which was tilted over one eye, Peta's face coloured hotly. In nervous fashion she touched her blue leather bag, staring at the clasp rather than at Noel.

'It's all so—so silly. It isn't that I want to get rid of you. But there's never been a question of anything else, has there?'

116

He took one of her hands—the one that wore his wedding-ring. His grey eyes were full of a deep regret. On an impulse he lifted that small, kind hand to his lips and kissed the ring.

'No—there hasn't,' he agreed. 'But I want you to know that *I* haven't the slightest wish to get rid of you.'

She was filled with embarrassment. Surely Noel Frensham didn't feel *that* way. But of course not, he was just being kind and flattering her. She drew the hand away, thankful that a nurse came into the ward to tell her that her car was waiting. A somewhat frigid announcement. Peta's action in leaving her newly-made 'husband' so soon after their marriage, and before he was really well, had been harshly criticised and she knew it. But she had lain herself open to criticism over this affair, and there was much more of it to be faced for both of them.

'Good-bye, Noel,' she said hurriedly, 'and mind you get strong and come home as fast as you can.'

'And will you promise me to be as happy in my house as you can until I come?'

'Thank you, I will.'

'Will you promise, too, that you won't—'

'Oh, I'll behave myself,' she broke in with a slight laugh. 'I know that's what you mean.'

He looked at her silently and intently. He meant so much more. But he must be content with the knowledge that she would, for her

117

own sake, be careful with Auburn Lyell. He could trust her. Any man could trust Peta. That was what made her so dear.

And the same impulse that had made him raise her hand to his lips, induced him to say:

'Kiss the poor sick husband good-bye.'

She gave a little laugh and bent over him. For an instant he shut his eyes and drew in a breath of the marvellous fragrance of her hair, some faint, delightful perfume which she used, and felt her cool lips against his cheek.

Then she was gone, and he turned his face to the pillow in an agony of jealousy which had hitherto never been his lot. He was in love with this young 'wife' of his—in love, and horribly, overwhelmingly jealous that she was going to England before him—going to London, where she would come under Auburn Lyell's spell again. He must follow and save her. He must get up, get about and take the first boat on to which he could walk. And until he rejoined her, he could only hope and pray that she would be all right.

CHAPTER NINE

The P. & O. boat on which Peta embarked at Port Said, docked at Tilbury on a glorious morning in mid-June.

The first person whom Peta saw when she

came down the gangway with a suit-case in her hand was Auburn Lyell standing beside a black and silver racing Bentley.

Her heart gave a wild leap at the sight of that graceful, handsome figure in grey flannels. He wore a dark green hat slightly on the side of the golden head which he held with that arrogant charm which never failed to draw the attention of women.

But the thrill of seeing him, of knowing that he had come to meet her in answer to her cable from the ship, was sadly tempered by the knowledge of what she had to tell him.

For the past ten days she had almost grown used to the name 'Mrs. Frensham.' But never used to the memory of what it entailed, and of her mad mistake in Port Said. Once the ship was away from the East, and from the very moment that they had come through the Bay of Biscay and neared the familiar coast-line of England, she had tried to feel that the whole thing was a fantastic dream which she could put a thousand miles behind her. But it didn't work. She was forced to the realisation that she had left a husband behind her in that hospital in Port Said. A man whom she did not love and with whom she would never live. But in the eyes of the law, *a husband*!

What would Auburn say? In an agony of doubt and anxiety she drew near him, shrinking from the prospect of making her necessary confession.

119

Auburn Lyell greeted her gaily, both hands outstretched. His one sensation in that moment was of pleasure in her appearance. She was browner than ever, slim and lovely in a suit, grey flannel, like his own, with a little red and white spot blouse; a floppy bow at the throat making her look ridiculously youthful. He had thought a great deal about her lately. And he was quite determined to break down any resistance which she might put up when he told her that he could not announce their engagement. The excuse he had ready was more genuine than his usual ones. It really would be impossible for him to marry a girl like Peta Marley.

Auburn had had a bit of a shock when he returned to business in London. Things were far from good. Present-day politics and the critical international situations were playing havoc with the business, with shares and finance in general. In fact, he was going to find himself hard up for a while.

Harder up than he had been since his wild days at Oxford when he had never been out of debt.

His father had told him that he could not continue to draw indiscriminately from the firm for his personal expenditure. He must go slow—very slow—that didn't suit Auburn. He might manage to keep his racing car and his motor-launch and have a decent time—but as a bachelor—not as a married man. Marriage was now further than ever from his mind.

Peta did not guess what was passing in his mind. The look in his eyes and the warmth in his voice, as he took her hands in his, were sufficient to make her confident of him.

'Baby-Heart!' he said in his slightly dramatic fashion. 'Oh, my sweet—it's heaven to see you!'

'Burn!' she whispered, dropped the suit-case and flung herself into his arms, regardless of the other people surging round them.

For a moment nothing mattered except the touch of his lips on hers and the frantic pounding of her heart. She was still quite dizzy and speechless with emotion when he took her arm and walked with her to the Customs, telling her how fit and brown and sweet she looked, and how incredibly dull London had seemed without her.

She let him talk on and kept silence until they were through the Customs and in the car and Auburn was steering it away from Tilbury *en route* for London.

It was luxurious and thrilling in the deep cushioned seat of the big Bentley which hummed and droned along the road, the silver bonnet flashing in the June sunlight. And it was good, she thought, to see England again, green meadows lush with buttercups, hedges starred with wild flowers, and little white clouds sailing across the blue sky. Such a pale, gentle blue after the exotic colours of the East.

Such a gracious, lovely England and such a fine world to have been in—if it wasn't for that ring on her left hand and that marriage certificate in her bag!

Auburn looked down at her thoughtful profile.

'You have the most adorable nose, sweetheart,' he said. 'Slightly tip-tilted and rather cheeky. But why is my Peta so quiet?'

She sighed.

'Oh, Burn, I don't know how I'm going to tell you!' broke from her.

Immediately he pulled the car up to the side of the road, switched off the engine, and drew his cigarette-case from his pocket.

'Oh ho! So Peta has a confession to make! Then she shall make it before we go an inch further. Have a cigarette, Beautiful, and don't look so tragic. If you've had a flirtation with some young subaltern on leave, or been kissed by a gallant major—I won't eat you up. I can't expect any girl with your mouth and eyes—and figure—to be ten days on board ship and not get involved in a moonlight love-affair.'

She tried to laugh but failed miserably.

'I wish it was only *that*!'

Auburn's eyes half closed. He hoped that Peta hadn't . . . but of course not . . . she wasn't that sort of girl. Her sweet youth and freshness were for him and he wasn't going to be disappointed.

'This sounds very serious, my Poppet. Out

with it. What have you done?'

She took off her hat and let the sun warm her hair. For an instant her dark, velvety eyes rested on her lover's face. Then she looked away from him. It was no use beating about the bush, she told herself. She must tell him and be done with it.

'You remember the . . . the sick doctor?'

'Do I not? Isn't he the cad that kept you away from me when we might have taken that plane together?'

Peta swallowed hard.

'Well, I . . . he . . .'

'My darling!' he broke in. 'You're not going to tell me that you had an affair in the hospital with a dying doctor!'

His flippancy jarred on her nerves which were already overstrained.

'Oh, do take me seriously, please, Burn. You don't know how hard this is for me to say.'

His brows went up. He lit his cigarette.

'Carry on. I'm all attention.'

So she told him word for word what had happened—all that she had been afraid to tell when they met in Port Said. He listened in amazement and with some dismay. He was neither amused nor pleased. But he was astonished. He had never for an instant imagined that little Peta would do anything so mad. To marry the man, believing that he was dying, just because he wanted to make a will in her favour! Well, if he had a lot of money it wasn't so silly, perhaps, and might have been grand if he pegged out. But as he had lived, it was a nice mess!

Auburn let Peta finish her story before he made any comment.

'You do believe that I wasn't in the least attracted by him and that I just regarded him as a friend, don't you?' were her final words. 'You must believe that, Burn, or I couldn't bear it! There was nothing between us—absolutely nothing.'

'H'm!' said Auburn Lyell. 'Well, it's difficult for me to believe that *he* wasn't attracted by *you.*'

'But he wasn't—it was just that he couldn't bear that nephew who was his next-of-kin, and that he thought I was alone in the world . . . and that I might benefit, and he wanted to repay me for being kind to him on board.'

She paused, breathlessly. Even as she said those words, she had a faint, uncomfortable memory of that moment of farewell with Noel Frensham when he had asked her to kiss him good-bye, and said:

'I want you to know that I haven't the slightest wish to get rid of you.'

She had wondered many times since if he had not been the least bit attracted by her.

'Well, it all sounds like a film story to me,' was Auburn's observation, 'and the maddest thing I've ever heard. Little fool, why didn't you tell me in Port Said?'

Peta's lips trembled.

'I was afraid . . . afraid of losing you.'

That flattered his vanity and he put a careless arm around her.

'My sweet, you should have more faith in my love than that.'

Those words took a great load off her mind. Impulsively she turned and pressed her cheek against his shoulder.

'Oh, Burn, darling, if you knew how terrified I've been to tell you this, in case it made a difference.'

'It only would if . . .'

'If you thought I had had an affair with Dr. Frensham . . . yes . . . I understand!' she broke in eagerly. 'But I haven't, and there was never any question of it, so I'm just what the novelists would call "a wife in name only".'

A load was then taken off Auburn's mind. He knew that he could believe implicitly every word that Peta said. The honesty and the whiteness of this girl were her chief attractions and appealed vastly to the *roué* in him.

Then he frowned sharply.

'Dr. *Frensham*, did you say?'

'Yes. Do you know him? I rather believe he knows you, or has heard of you.'

Auburn Lyell sat still and the arm about her shoulders stiffened imperceptibly. The faintest colour tinged the tan in his cheeks. He had that very fair skin which flushed easily and gave him a boyish, self-conscious air which was entirely spurious. He was incapable of shame.

'*Noel* Frensham?' he questioned.

'So you do know him.'

'I've heard of him,' said Auburn abruptly. 'What did he say about me?'

'Nothing—just that he'd heard of you.'

Auburn looked relieved. He wouldn't have been at all pleased had the story of Toni Maitland been dragged to the light for Peta's benefit. What a confoundedly small world it was! Fancy Peta getting herself mixed up with that fellow, of all the doctors in the world . . . the heart specialist into whose Home poor Toni had been sent!

But why worry? He had no reason to believe that Frensham knew Toni's story or connected him, Lyell, with it. At any rate, Auburn wasn't going to bother about that. Toni was a ghost of the past, and Peta was a warm living presence at his side and a very attractive one.

She lifted her dark, soft eyes to his.

'Will you forgive me, Burn? I'm in a dreadful mess-up, but I'm going to get free. He's going to let me divorce him. I'll tell you what he says . . .'

And there followed Peta's explanation of the present position, of why an annulment would be difficult and unpleasant, and of Noel's suggestion for getting her out of the difficulty.

'You can see what a fine person he is, Burn. He's prepared to suffer loss of reputation and everything else, and I must say I admire him for that.'

'Anybody would have done the same,' said Auburn stiffly, having no desire for Peta to admire any man but himself.

'Well, anyhow, he won't trouble me. As soon as he gets back to London, he's fixing this divorce.'

'And you're to go to his house in Wimpole Street as "Mrs. Frensham" until then, are you?'

'He says so. Burn, don't be angry about it. I've been an awful little fool, but . . .'

'I'm not in the least angry,' he cut in, and gathered her in his arms. 'I adore you and this isn't going to matter the very least. It just means that we must postpone our—engagement— until you're free.'

Her spirits soared. She felt an immense love for him flooding her. He was marvellous, understanding, everything that she had ever thought him. She told him so whilst Auburn Lyell's thin, rather cruel fingers toyed with her brown curls and his lip took on a queer satirical twist.

This was beginning to be amusing, now that he had got over the first shock of Peta's confession. He had lost nothing by her absurd marriage to Noel Frensham. Indeed, he had gained a lot. Gained the time which he wanted in order to complete his conquest of Peta without tying himself down to her. He needn't

127

tell her that he was hard up and that affairs were very tight in the business. Everything fitted in beautifully. There could be no question of announcing their engagement now. This divorce would take six months to go through, and meanwhile he and Peta could have the hell of a good time, he thought.

It suited him admirably that she should be a 'wife in name only,' mistress of a large West End house, spending Frensham's money. And there was more than that to be gained. Peta had said that of course she wouldn't touch the third of Frensham's income to which she would be entitled, and Auburn let her imagine that he entirely agreed. But he meant to find out just what sort of income Frensham had. These big specialists made a lot of money, and from what Peta told him about the shooting-box in Scotland, and Frensham's annual trips out East, his big game hunting, etc., it sounded as though he had private means, too. Plenty of this world's goods. That was why he had married Peta, and made a will in her favour. He was in love with her, no doubt. Well, that didn't matter to Auburn. Peta was crazily in love with *him*. If finances didn't improve at home, and Peta was well-off, he might even consider marrying her. That was all in the air. Meanwhile he could have a lot of fun with her before taking any drastic steps.

Peta read none of the thoughts that flitted through his plastic mind. He spent the next few minutes making love to her in his inimitable fashion, and it left her in no doubt that he was more than ever in love with her. He believed everything she had to say, he assured her, and would be her devoted slave until she was free from the absurd marriage.

They sped up the London road, Peta snuggled against his side, one hand locked in his. She felt that there was no more reason to be unhappy or worried. Auburn was marvellous. His gaiety, his high spirits infected her until she felt utterly gay herself, and confident that everything was going to be all right. Auburn even succeeded in making her look forward to the next few weeks when she must pose as Mrs. Frensham.

'It'll be fun,' he said, 'and I'll come and call and take you out.'

'But we'll have to be careful, darling. Because I've got to divorce Noel, you know . . .'

'Oh, we'll be angelic!' he said airily. 'But I'm going to see you—every day. That fellow may be your husband by law, but he isn't going to tell my girl what she may or may not do.'

Peta sighed happily.

'Of course he won't. And I want you to meet him and be friends with him, because he's frightfully nice, Burn, and you must say he's treating me very handsomely.'

Auburn nodded, but he had nothing to say. He wasn't sure that he wanted to meet or make friends with Dr. Frensham.

The rest of that day teemed with excitement for Peta—it was so exciting, indeed, that she had little time in which to regret what she had done in Port Said. Indeed, Auburn's unswerving attentions as a lover made her feel that she had nothing to regret and that it was only poor Noel Frensham now who was going to get the worst of this deal. She decided that she must be very nice to him when they met again and make things as easy as she could for him.

Auburn drove her to the house in Wimpole Street and left her there. They agreed that it would be best for her to introduce herself to the household without him being with her.

But later he would come and fetch her, take her out to dinner and a show. They must, he said, spend this evening together and have a good time while they could. It wouldn't hurt her reputation. He would see to that, he said. But he wanted to be with her as much as possible before Dr. Frensham came home. So Peta, with only one desire in her heart—to be with her lover—needed little persuading, and feeling more light-hearted than she had expected, stepped out of the Bentley and walked up to that door which bore the brass plate inscribed with *Dr. N. C. Frensham, M.D.,* and rang the bell.

CHAPTER TEN

About ten days later Peta sat at a walnut bureau in her boudoir, the windows of which looked down upon Wimpole Street, and paused to read a letter which she had been busily writing—a letter to Noel which she was having to rush through in order to catch the air mail. She had left it so long. She disliked writing to Noel. But she had done so dutifully every other day, in answer to his brief pencilled scrawls, each one of which begged for news.

There was so much news, and yet so little to give. For the person who occupied most of her time and thoughts was Auburn, and a certain delicacy of feeling forbade that she should mention Auburn in any of her letters to Noel Frensham.

She had seen her lover every day—sometimes twice a day. He was enchanting and attentive, taking her out to teas and dinners, to shows and suppers, teaching her to dance with him, drive his car, drink cocktails; in fact, to become a most sophisticated 'young woman about town.' All of which left her rather breathless and bewildered, although very much the same Peta deep down inside. A rather shy, peace-loving Peta with more simple tastes than the girl that Auburn seemed to want to make of her.

But of course, she told herself, since she was to marry him she must allow him to mould her into the shape that he desired. She adored him and she was having a 'marvellous time'—so what matter if she was a trifle tired, not looking as well as when she came off that boat, and a little nervy from the continued racketing, the gay round of Mayfair with Auburn—too many late nights. And a little afraid, not so much of Auburn as of herself and the terrific influence that he had over her.

Sometimes, when she thought about it sanely and calmly, she wondered if it was right to allow any man to take such complete possession of her heart. And then as soon as she met Auburn again she stopped worrying and told herself that one day she would be his wife, and it was quite fitting and proper that he should live completely in her mind and heart.

She sat back in her chair and read over the last sheet of notepaper which was on her blotter.

'It still seems strange and hopelessly wrong for me to be living here as your wife. The servants are all frightfully nice and attentive to me. Mrs. McLeod is grand, and they all seem to adore you. But I suppose they must think it queer that I should have arrived here by myself and left you ill out there. You can't think how anxious I am for

132

you to come back and end it all.'

Peta's red lips tightened as she read those last words. They seemed ungrateful, but she really did not enjoy her role as Mrs. Frensham. It made her feel guilty and beastly. And it was quite true—she was unutterably anxious for Noel to come back and set her free.

These last ten days had flown by and it was still as though she lived a fantastic dream, and that some time or other she *would* wake up and find herself Peta Marley again—the Peta who had been Derek Bradley's nursery-governess.

She let her gaze wander round the boudoir which had, so the housekeeper told her, belonged to Noel's mother. It was one of the smallest rooms in the big solemn house, and furnished like the others, in exquisite taste. Everything was old and rare and full of dignity. There had been hours when Peta was not able to be with Auburn, which she had spent in admiring all these things which appealed to her. The sort of things for which she had always hankered and which her own family had not been able to afford.

The late Mrs. Frensham, so the housekeeper told her, was an authority on antiques, and a collector in her fashion. She had lived in this house since Noel was a boy and his father, a noted physician in his day, had practised here as Noel was now doing.

This little room Peta used was still full of Mary Frensham's personality, which must, Peta realised, have been a very gracious one. It was reflected in her choice of Queen Anne walnut, polished to a dark gold, in the rich wines and blues and ambers of old Persian rugs, in the beauty of Italian brocaded curtains, soft faded rose embroidered with threads of gold, and there was old china, rose and white and blue against the panelled walls, exquisite miniatures, and an enchanting period mirror with two candlesticks, in which, Peta had been told, Noel's mother burnt candles only on her son's birthday. She had bought that mirror with the gilt candlesticks the week that he was born.

A charming story, Peta had heard about those candles and the sacred rite of burning them all through the years, in celebration of a little boy's birthday. And later, even when Noel had become a man, and right up to the days when Mrs. Frensham grew too feeble to light them herself, she had ordered the candles to be lit, that particular day in June, in honour of her only idolised son.

Peta could imagine how lonely it must have been for Noel when his mother died. There was altogether an atmosphere of loneliness in the big house which affected Peta, who was sensitive to such things. There was nothing modern or gay about it and yet Peta felt that had she been really concerned in the matter, she would not have altered the rooms any more than Noel had done. They were all lovely. Perhaps it was the loneliness that upset her and made her glad to get away with Auburn to something bright and gay. On the other hand, she could not entirely share Auburn's love of the ultra-modern—of chromium, strip-lighting, built-in furniture, all the cold hardness of such decoration.

There was something about this house which suggested home. Peta could understand now why Noel loved it and had not wanted to leave it to an indifferent nephew, belonging to a generation which could not understand the peace or dignity of a bygone age. An age in which Peta believed she would have liked to live, although she had never suggested such a thing to Auburn, because he would not have understood.

Yes, under different circumstances Peta might have loved this house and all that was in it. But now it seemed to her a place in which she had no right and which she must get out of as soon as possible.

She had learnt much about Noel while she had been here. The members of his staff could not say enough about him . . . his goodness, his greatness, his generosity as well as his fine work as a doctor. And she had received a touching welcome from them all, in spite of the fact that they must think it strange that she should have come here alone, and was always going out with another man. One and all, whenever they saw her, they asked for news of 'the doctor,' and when he would be coming back.

Yesterday, when Peta had told the housekeeper that the latest bulletin from Port Said was good, the old woman had embarrassed her by saying:

'That's grand, and when the doctor's back, madam, we must see about moving you from the little room you have now into the big double one.'

Peta had hurriedly told her that she wished to keep her own room, and that the doctor would keep his. But she had seen a look of surprise, if not of disappointment, behind the old woman's spectacles. It was obviously a blow to her romantic notions. Well, there would be many more of these blows which must be administered right and left once Noel got back. Everybody in the house would be upset to think that Noel's marriage was to be dissolved whilst in its infancy . . . And none of them would understand their adored doctor behaving so badly. It certainly was grossly unfair on Noel, and it seemed almost sacrilege to bring the ugly atmosphere of impending divorce into this gracious, kindly house. But what else was there to do? Whenever Peta thought about it she worried . . . but in fairness to herself, she knew that the thing must go through, because it would be equally wrong to spoil her life just through that mistaken act of generosity to a man whom she thought was dying.

She wondered, sometimes, if she lacked in feeling for Auburn when she worried about the whole thing, for he exhibited a divine indifference to anything, anyone but themselves. It was obvious egotism on his part, but she could forgive it easily because he wanted nothing but her, he said. And how could she be cross with him for *that*?

She finished the letter to Noel, and addressed it. Then her gaze fell on a note which lay open on the desk. It was from Edith Powell, Noel's sister, and the mother of young Kenneth who had expected to be his uncle's heir.

Peta had not seen any of the Powells yet. She had avoided the meeting, because she thought it futile to introduce herself to Noel's relations and friends since she was so soon to relinquish her place at his side. But Mrs. Powell lived in London, and was being insistent, and had announced, in this note, her intention of calling at the house this afternoon. No doubt she was furious that her boy had been deposed, and she wished to see her brother's mysterious, newly-married wife, whose advent was an unexpected blow. Noel had been regarded as a confirmed bachelor.

It was all very awkward, Peta thought, and the sooner it was over the better.

Then yesterday there had been an awkward hour with Mrs. Bradley. Mary Bradley, having recovered from the first shock of learning that her young nursery-governess had stepped off the boat at Port Said and married a dying doctor who hadn't died, was all for Peta remaining married to Noel. She had argued with her yesterday, that she was a little fool to throw up what appeared to be an excellent marriage—for Auburn Lyell. And when Peta had said, proudly, that she preferred to marry Auburn, Mary Bradley had become silent and a little sinister about the whole affair, as though she doubted whether Peta would ever realise her ambition.

It made Peta furious, but when Mrs. Bradley had gone, she had thought it over, and decided that it was not only disloyalty but jealousy on Mary Bradley's part. She had always had a 'soft spot' for Auburn herself. Well, nothing that she or anybody else could say would make Peta give Auburn up as long as he loved and wanted her. And why, in any case, she asked herself, should she stay married to a man who was still a mere stranger to her, and who could never mean anything more in her life?

There came a double tap on the boudoir door—a signal, with which Peta had grown familiar. Mrs. McLeod was outside. Dear old Mrs. McLeod, who had been housekeeper in the Frensham family for over forty years.

She came in looking just as she must have

138

looked when Noel was a little boy, Peta thought. Plump, well corseted, wearing a black merino dress which had almost a bustle effect and with little starched white linen collar and cuffs, and the keys of her house dangling from her belt. Mrs. McLeod was nearing seventy, but still a magnificent guardian of the staff, the linen cupboard, and the dozen and one little details which made Noel's house run on oiled wheels.

She brought a telegram for Peta and handed it to her in respectful silence. While the girl opened it the old woman eyed her through the thick lens of her glasses and puzzled, not for the first time, over this marriage which Mr. Noel had made. He was still 'Mr. Noel' to her. It was not easy for her to think of him as 'the doctor', which name had belonged to his father before him, in this very house. Why had Mr. Noel married this slip of a girl so suddenly, out in foreign parts, then sent her home before him? Ay, and why did she go out so much with that young gentleman who was handsome and pleasant enough, but it was not the fitting thing for a young bride who had the best husband in the world. It was all very confusing to Mrs. McLeod. Not that she disliked 'Mrs. Noel.' She thought her a gentle bonnie wee girl, and far from being one of these modern hussies Mrs. McLeod had dreaded when she first read Mr. Noel's letter announcing his sudden marriage.

Peta looked up from the wire with a flushed face.

'Gracious!' she exclaimed childishly. 'Dr. Frensham is arriving tonight.'

'Tonight!' echoed Mrs. McLeod. 'Och—what a surprise!'

'He's flying back. I'm sure he oughtn't to. I don't think he's strong enough. He must have made up his mind in a great hurry.'

'Bless his heart, madam, and yours too,' said Mrs. McLeod piously. 'It will be a gr-r-rand reunion between husband and wife.'

Peta looked from the housekeeper to the telegram in her hand. Her brows came together and she gave a little nervous sigh. There would be no grand reunion! How horribly embarrassing it all was! There was only one good thing about it. Once Noel was home they could set about securing the divorce.

She looked at her watch. It was nearly lunch time. She had better phone Auburn at his office. It wouldn't be good news to him. He had arranged to take her out this evening, and of course she would have to put that off.

She heard Mrs. McLeod's soft Scottish voice:

'Oh, weel, I'd better be seeing about preparing for the doctor. You say he's to have his own room, and you'll be keeping yours?'

'Yes,' said Peta, and her cheeks went hot again. She liked old Mrs. McLeod, but wished the old dear would not harp on this bedroom business. It seemed to upset her badly that she couldn't prepare the big double bedroom which had been occupied by Noel's father and mother.

A few moments later, having listened dutifully to Mrs. McLeod's enthusiastic plans for giving the doctor his favourite dinner, and having red roses, his favourite flowers, arranged in the house, Peta telephoned to her lover.

As she had anticipated, Auburn received the news that Noel was unexpectedly returning home none too favourably.

'But you won't cut your dinner with me, Beautiful, will you?'

'I must, Burn. I can't very well be out when he arrives.'

'Look here, you can't start the dutiful wife stunt, darling.'

'Of course not, stupid, but I must be ordinarily polite.'

Auburn whistled.

'Phew! That's a crack at me, my sweet, but I shall certainly quarrel with you if you let even politeness prevent you from seeing me.'

Peta gave a warm, excited little laugh. He always excited her, always managed by some perfectly charming speech to prevent her from resenting the most outrageous things that he said.

'Darling, you know how much I want to see

you.'

'Then come out with me tonight. The fellow can't expect you to hang round and wait for him to turn up.'

She wanted to go. There was nothing she wanted more. Going out with Auburn meant an intimate little meal at one of his pet restaurants, then perhaps a show, coming back in his car, and he stealing in here for a few moments to say good night . . . to hold her close and long, make her dizzy with his kisses . . . kiss her until she had to force herself to be sane and send him away, terrified of her own utter longing for him. All so sweet and dangerous. A danger to be averted, because they must both be circumspect and patient at the present time. But one day she would be free, and he would marry her, and then there would be no need to say good-bye.

'Darling, I'm crazy to see you, but I simply must be here tonight,' she said. 'It would look so peculiar and we've got to be sensible until the divorce is through.'

Auburn argued and grumbled, then grew slightly sarcastic. It was obvious, he said, that he was going to be asked to 'snoop' round like a dog, and wait for a bone to be flung to him, once this 'damn doctor' got back. He was fed up with it. He didn't see why Peta should be so sensible. He hated sensible people. And so on, until Peta was upset. Auburn was, sometimes, quite unreasonable and difficult. She had to admit it. And he didn't seem to have any instinct about 'doing the right thing,' which puzzled her. Before the telephone conversation ended he had 'forgiven her,' he said, and would ring her up tomorrow to see how the land lay.

Peta put the telephone down, wondering what she had done that had to be 'forgiven,' and feeling rather miserable. It was bad enough having to put Burn off, and face the strain of Noel's return, without Burn being difficult. She grew more miserable as the day went by, and felt a really acute longing to see Auburn, to make sure that he wasn't really cross with her, feel the reassurance of his lips and arms. But she had to conquer the longing.

She had no idea what time to expect Noel. At half-past six he had not yet turned up. She went to her bedroom and changed into one of the chiffon evening dresses which she had taken out to India. She had bought no new clothes since then. She was well aware that she did not look really smart enough for Auburn's liking—nor, perhaps, for her position in this important household. But she refused to spend Noel's money and had none of her own.

The atmosphere of the said household was getting on her nerves tonight. There were such rushings about, such whisperings and bustlings—the whole staff in a state of upheaval, headed by Mrs. McLeod, all of thcm delighted at the prospect of the doctor's return. He was certainly a great favourite, Peta

143

thought.

Miss Turner, his secretary, had only just gone, having left a message that she would be here at the usual time in the morning to take the doctor's orders for the day. Although, she said, she did not suppose he would go back to work until he was quite strong again.

There were red roses in the consulting-room and the library, which was a small, oak-panelled room full of books, which Noel used to sit in, preferring it to the big formal drawing-room. There were roses all over the house.

Then just before Peta had her bath Mrs. McLeod came upstairs, breathless and emotional, to tell 'Mrs. Frensham' that she had just remembered that today was the doctor's birthday. He was arriving home on his very birthday, she said, and it must be made a double celebration.

Peta could not be otherwise than impressed by the general preparations for Noel's return. But she felt hopelessly embarrassed at the thought of meeting him, of having to act her role as his wife. It was all so difficult when she was madly in love with another man. Acting, in any case, was foreign to her nature, which was essentially a frank and simple one. She did not imagine it would be any better for Noel. She decided to try not to be too egotistical tonight, in spite of Auburn's reverse idea, and to put up some sort of show of welcome for poor Noel. After all he had been very decent to her, and here she was living in his house, and having what she would have thought in the old days a very easy time of it.

When she was ready she looked at her reflection in the mirror. She knew that she looked nice in that rose and white chiffon dress, and she pinned two of the red roses which Mrs. McLeod had given her on her shoulder, and decided that she was now quite festive enough. She must just try to cultivate a more festive expression before Noel arrived. But every time she heard a car roll down Wimpole Street, her heart thumped with dread lest it should be 'the doctor' arriving.

She walked into her boudoir to find a cigarette. She stood a moment deep in thought in front of the fireplace, smoking. Then her gaze lit on the wax candles in front of the gilt mirror, and there flashed through her brain the memory of the story that Mrs. McLeod had told her. Noel's mother had always lit these candles on Noel's birthday. Always. There was nobody to do it for him now. And it was the sort of little, sentimental custom that a man would miss.

The sentimentalist in Peta stirred. On an impulse she took a match, lit the candles and stood back to admire the effect. How charming they looked, so slender and cream coloured, tapering to little gold spears of light, reflected in the old mirror.

She heard a door slam and reverberate

through the house, then voices below. A man's familiar voice in particular. Peta, with every nerve a-quiver and her hands growing cold with nerves, ran to the window and looked down. The warm June evening was still light. London looked serene and lovely under a miraculous sky of that rather deep tranquil blue peculiar to a summer night.

She saw a car outside the house and a man-servant unstrapping some luggage, and she knew that Noel had come.

She walked back into the room feeling ridiculously awkward. What did one do on such an occasion? A nice little wife would run down to meet her husband. But she wasn't a nice little wife. She was just a stranger whom he had married quite by mistake. She stood smoking her cigarette, her whole body trembling with sheer nervousness.

CHAPTER ELEVEN

Noel must have asked Mrs. McLeod where Peta was and been told, because while she still stood in the boudoir brooding over things, he came upstairs and found her. He took the stairs slowly. He was still not very strong. But he was extraordinarily eager to see this wife of his. It was so delightful to know that she was waiting for him, and to have heard Mrs.

McLeod say that 'the young mistress' was at home, was very well and 'looking bonnie.'

Peta, the mistress of his home, and mistress of his heart as well, he told himself ruefully, because it was knocking far too emotionally when he opened the boudoir door and saw her standing there, looking so lovely in her rose and white evening dress which he remembered her wearing on board ship, when she had been so kind to him.

'Hullo!' he said, and tried to make his voice sound ordinary. But he was filled with the desire to snatch her in his arms and tell her how much he had looked forward to this meeting; tell her that she had never been out of his thoughts since she had left Port Said, and that although she had never mentioned Auburn Lyell in any of her letters to him, he had been torn with jealousy and wondered how many times she had met the man.

'Hullo,' said Peta, and she, too, tried to be ordinary, and added a few formal words to the effect that she hoped he had quite recovered from his illness. To which Noel replied that he was a new man and that a few weeks' holiday in England would soon restore him to his old fine state of health.

'I needn't ask how you are—you look splendid,' he said. 'And of course—'

He stopped. Peta saw his gaze wander over her to the candlesticks. And she saw his face, still thin and delicate from his recent illness, flush scarlet, then grow quite pale. He turned to her.

'Who lit those?' he asked abruptly.

Peta's fingers played with the pearl necklace which she was wearing. She gave a nervous laugh.

'I did. I—'

'Why?' he interrupted.

'I hope you aren't cross,' she said. 'Perhaps it was foolish of me, but I—Mrs. McLeod told me that they used always to be lit for your birthday. It is your birthday today, isn't it?'

'Yes,' he said.

He spoke in a hushed voice. And the look in his eyes disconcerted her. It was a warm, solemn, rather intimate expression which, somehow, she felt she had no right to see. A look that belonged to his dead mother—and not to her.

He drew nearer Peta.

'My mother used to light those candles on my birthday because she bought that mirror just before I was born and somehow always connected it with me. It was sentimental of her, but she took things like that seriously. I appreciated it because it was a fond and foolish sign of what she felt for me. I was devoted to my mother.'

'I know,' said Peta.

His gaze returned to the candles and there was an instant's silence. He was more moved than he had believed possible by the sight of

148

those candles burning to welcome him on his return. And to know that Peta had lit them. She had a strong romantic vein running through her. But why she had done this he could not quite fathom, unless it was just a whim on her part.

'What made you light them?' he asked.

Her lashes dropped.

'I don't know. Just that . . . that Mrs. McLeod told me it was your birthday and I thought you'd like the candles lit.'

'I do very much. It's the first time they've been lit since my mother died. I've missed it. It was very, very charming of you, Peta. I daresay I seem rather stupid and emotional to you, but thank you, my dear. Thanks a lot.'

He took her right hand, kissed it and dropped it again. She was overcome with embarrassment and said nothing. But she thought:

'Funny . . . a little thing like this touching a man so deeply . . . but of course, it is the little, intimate things that touch one in this life. I understand, and I rather like it in Noel.'

Curiously enough her thoughts strayed to Auburn in this moment. She found herself wishing that he had a shred of such feeling in him. He was marvellous, he was tender and and passionate by turns, all that any woman wanted . . . it was disloyal of her to find the slightest fault with him . . . yet she couldn't be blind to the fact that there was *something*

149

missing in Auburn. Sometimes it was plainer to her than at others. Little sentimental things bored him, left him cold. The episode of these candles for instance, he would treat with derision, she was sure.

Noel said:

'I'm rather lucky to have found such a delightful welcome. I'd almost decided to stop celebrating my birthday. I'm an old man. Forty today.'

'You don't look it,' said Peta.

She meant it. She was struck by something peculiarly boyish about Noel this evening. Perhaps it was that new air of fragility. There were so few grey threads in the darkness of his hair, and his figure was slim and upright. Only his eyes were the eyes of a man who had seen 'life' and lived it. And there was that faintly cynical curve to his finely cut lips. She remembered how on board, when she had first met him, she had noticed that he had a charming voice and beautifully shaped hands. Oh yes, Noel Frensham was a very attractive man, and no doubt the hero of his numerous women patients. And there was something remote and lonely about him which she had also noticed in the beginning of their friendship. It would have been lonely for him coming back here tonight, with just the servants to welcome him, and express thankfulness for his recovery. Peta was quite glad she had stayed in tonight. She thawed to him.

'I believe you've got a real birthday dinner, too,' she said. 'Mrs. McLeod has been fussing about ever since your wire arrived.'

He sat down on the edge of a chair.

'Let's ring for some sherry and drink it here. At least, have I your permission to drink a glass of sherry in your boudoir?'

She laughed and rang the bell.

'Of course.'

'I want to know how you've been getting on, and how you like living here.'

'I like it very much,' she said politely. 'And I think it's a glorious house full of glorious things.'

'You seem to have endeared yourself to Mackie.'

'You mean Mrs. McLeod?'

'Yes. She's been Mackie to me since I was a kid.'

'She's a grand old woman and we get on very well,' said Peta.

'You haven't found it too depressing?'

Peta played with her necklace again and avoided his gaze.

'No.'

But he imagined he could read her thoughts and he shook his head at her.

'Yes you have. You've been rather depressed. It's quiet and gloomy for you here, perhaps. Mackie's old and Miss Turner isn't young. The place needs a bit of brightening up. I know it, but I've always been too busy at the hospital and with my patients to worry about such things. But it strikes home tonight. It's so very nice to find you here, my dear.'

'Thank you,' said Peta a trifle stiffly, not knowing what else to say.

The sherry was brought in. They poured it out, lit cigarettes, drank and talked for a few moments on an impersonal note.

Noel described his last week at the hospital and what the doctors had said about him, and what a lot he owed to that Egyptian who had helped save his life. He asked if Peta had seen his sister, and Peta told him that Mrs. Powell had threatened to call this very day, but had put off the call.

'Fortunately,' Peta said, 'because I really don't want to meet her. It would be so embarrassing.'

Noel leaned back in an arm-chair, sipped his sherry, and through the faint spiral of his cigarette smoke, looked at the slim girl in her rose and white chiffons and felt absurdly contented and at ease. He had much to be thankful for tonight. After all, he had nearly died out there in Port Said. It was pretty good to feel well again, to be back in old England, in his London home with his work awaiting him. To be sitting here this warm June night in his mother's boudoir with the birthday candles burning as of old . . . and Peta to welcome him. God! if only he stood a chance with her and it wasn't necessary to put through that damn divorce.

The moment which Peta dreaded arrived. He began to question her about herself.

'I hope you've done what I told you and bought yourself some clothes, and had a good time,' he said.

She told him with a touch of pride which he found quaint and delightful, that she hadn't spent any money and certainly had not bought new clothes.

'I wouldn't be in the least justified in making free use of your money,' she said.

'Oh yes, you would,' he said. 'After all, I've taken you from your job.'

She made a little gesture.

'But I'd rather not spend your money. It's been quite enough . . . living here . . . taking your hospitality.'

His lips twisted. He looked at her left hand and with a touch of pleasure saw that she still wore his wedding ring.

'That sounds wrong. After all, my wife shouldn't regard it as taking my hospitality, living in the home that is legally hers.'

Peta moved uncomfortably. He said those words 'my wife' in quite a possessive manner.

'Legally, yes, but nothing more,' she reminded him.

He bit his lip.

'You still hate the position violently?'

'I want to be free.'

He leaned forward and flung his cigarette-end into the fireplace and interlaced his fingers.

'Have you seen a lot of—him?'

'Auburn, you mean?'

'Yes.'

'Quite a lot,' she admitted, her cheeks hot and pink. 'Every day, in fact. I've been out with him. I don't suppose that matters. The divorce hasn't started.'

He gave her a long queer look.

'And how did he take the news of your marriage to me?'

'He didn't like it, of course, but he understands—absolutely. He's been wonderful.'

'Has he taken you to see his people?'

'No, he can't very well do that now. He says we must wait until I'm free.'

'What guarantee have you that he'll marry you then?'

She stared at him.

'But of course he will!'

'What guarantee have you?' repeated Noel.

'I don't know what you mean. One has no guarantee for that sort of thing except that one knows—one knows—' She broke off with a gesture, her cheeks peony red.

Noel's eyes half closed. He stared beyond her. He was seeing, not this pretty, flushed, impulsive young wife of his, but that broken girl who had died with her hand in his telling him that she had loved Auburn Lyell so much—too *much*.

'One never knows, Peta,' he said, 'and particularly not with men like Lyell.'

Peta went white.

'That's insulting.'

'It may sound so, but if you knew as much about Lyell as I do, you'd realise that one couldn't insult him—unless the truth is an insult.'

There was an instant's frozen silence. Peta's large brown eyes stared at him with mixed anger and dismay. He hated to see her look white, like that, and to know what dreadful power the man had over her. He had not meant that this first evening home should be anything like this, nor did he wish the 'reunion' to develop into a sordid row. But he had gone too far. There broke from Peta's lips a torrent of words, furious, reproachful, questioning.

How dared he say such a thing, she demanded. He didn't know Auburn. Auburn had heard of him but had never met him. And what object had Noel in making such remarks, or in suggesting that she needed any *guarantee* other than Auburn's word that he loved her and wished to marry her? She wouldn't remain in the room and hear Auburn spoken of in such a way. And so on until Noel held up a hand and silenced her.

'Don't go on, my dear. It's no good. I can see that it's quite useless for me to appeal to your intelligence over this.'

Peta could scarcely believe her ears.

'Appeal to my intelligence!' she exclaimed. 'What has intelligence got to do with it? You've insinuated that Auburn is—is so bad that nothing would be too insulting for him. It doesn't require any intellect to understand *that*! I think you must be mad.'

He passed a hand over his forehead. He was feeling very tired now, exhausted by the air journey, and the excitement of the return home.

'Oh, God,' he thought. 'If only that man didn't hold her in the hollow of his hand! If only I could make her see what he is, without driving her further and further from me.'

He knew that he wanted more than anything to keep her, hold her to his heart and never let her go. Yet, for her sake, he must go on with the truth—the truth that would make her bitterly resentful.

'Listen, my dear,' he said wearily. 'I'm not mad, but when I say that I think it useless appealing to your intelligence, I mean that you obviously won't give me a fair hearing, or admit that anything that I say is justified, because you're so blindly in love with this man.'

That made her a trifle uneasy. She calmed down.

'I'm quite willing to be fair, but I don't think any woman in love would stand hearing horrible things said about her lover.'

'No,' Noel said with a faint smile. 'You're

156

very loyal. So much more loyal than he deserves.'

That made her angry again.

'Don't keep running him down. What do you know about him. What *do* you know?'

'Quite a lot.'

'Then I'll ask him to come here and see you, and you can say it to him.'

Noel shrugged his shoulders.

'He'd deny everything. It would only be a question of his word against mine.'

Curiosity, that most human instinct in every woman, stirred within Peta. She looked at Noel through her thick lashes and said:

'What do you know? You've never met him.'

'I've come in contact with him indirectly and heard as much as I want to know. I'll tell you the story, but not now. I'm much too tired.'

'I'm sorry,' she said coldly. 'Of course, you've had a long journey, and you're not strong yet. Perhaps you'd better go to bed and rest.'

He gave her a queer baffling smile.

'Not yet. First of all I want this birthday dinner. You did say there was one, didn't you?'

'Yes,' she said grudgingly.

He stood up and put a hand on her shoulder.

'Don't be furious with me, Peta, because I'm trying to help you, if you but knew it.'

She tapped the point of a small slipper against the floor.

157

'I don't see how it's helping me to make dark insinuations against the man I'm in love with.'

He drew a deep sigh.

'You believe in him implicitly?'

'I do.'

'Was he introduced to you with a perfect reputation?'

She bit her lip. She had a faint recollection of the things that Mary Bradley had said out in India. Things suggesting that Auburn was a bad flirt. Well, perhaps that was true. Burn was so very handsome and attractive. He must have had a few affairs. But men like that often met the right girl, settled down and made excellent husbands. He had asked her to marry him, and what had he to gain by it if he didn't love her? She wouldn't have a penny. She wouldn't take anything that Noel Frensham offered. She was confident of Burn's love for her. She felt infuriated with Noel because he suggested anything to the contrary.

Noel was saying:

'Never mind. Don't bother to answer. Perhaps I'll deal with Mr. Lyell instead of with you.'

She gave a short laugh.

'Yes, I think it's best for you to see Auburn and say all these things to him.'

Her voice was hard. Her young lovely face was hard. Frensham had a moment of hopeless depression. He was badly in love now and he knew it. He remembered her as she had been on board, so soft and kindly. And he knew that there were sweet, kind instincts in her. Those candles . . . they were burning in honour of his birthday and she had lit them . . . like his mother had done. He did not want her to look so hard and be so hard, and all because of that insufferable inhuman fellow, Auburn Lyell!

It would have been hard to lose her under any condition, but how much easier, he told himself bitterly, it would have been to hand her over to a man worthy of her love.

'Peta,' he said very gently, 'can we forget about Auburn Lyell just for the moment and have our dinner together as friends?'

It cost her an effort to meet him half-way. She felt rebellious and resentful because he attempted to belittle the man she loved. Then a new thought struck her. Perhaps Noel was jealous. Yes, perhaps he was running Auburn down because he was jealous of him. Out in Port Said he had seemed to want to keep her for himself. That was rather flattering. No woman could be angry with a man who was jealous. She could only pity him. Burn had suggested that the doctor was in love with her. She had repudiated it at the time. She had not been vain enough to imagine that a man as clever, as rich, as attractive in his way as Noel Frensham, should be in love with her. She decided to forgive him the silly things he said about Auburn. Of course they *were* silly and

Auburn would soon allay any doubts that Noel chose to plant in her mind. Not that she did doubt Burn for a moment.

She said, on a softer note:

'All right, we'll forget about it and have dinner.'

He breathed again. The last thing he wanted was to come out with the story of Toni Maitland, tonight.

He put an arm through Peta's and walked with her to the door.

'You've given me such a lovely birthday present by lighting my candles and being here to dine with me,' he said, 'and I am grateful, truly I am.'

'Oh, that's all right,' she said awkwardly.

They were talking on a friendly note when they got downstairs. And Peta found the mother instinct in her stirring at the sight of his thin, almost gaunt face, and the appealing melancholy in his eyes. He still looked very ill. She fussed over him a bit. She made them bring a cushion to put at his back when at length they sat at the big mahogany table which gleamed with cut glass and shining Georgian silver in the beautiful Adams dining-room. The perfect little meal thought out by 'Mackie' was served to them, and iced hock brought for Peta. But she made Noel drink a strong whisky-and-soda, then drank the hock herself to give him a birthday toast. She forgot her antagonism. And she looked so lovely

160

sitting there at the foot of his table, opposite him, her face framed by tall green candles, the soft light reflected in her great brown eyes, that it both enchanted and agonised him to see her there. It was almost more than he could endure to think that she wanted to give herself, body and soul, to Auburn Lyell.

He tried to entertain her with various anecdotes which he thought might interest her. She liked to hear about his hunting elephant in India. She had made him tell her about it on board when they first met. And she liked stories about his place in Scotland and Jonnie, his Cairn terrier.

'You were going to look after Jonnie for me if I'd died, weren't you?' he asked with a faint smile.

She nodded.

'I'm awfully fond of dogs and the country.'

'I'm thinking of going up to my place in Scotland in a few days for a change of air. It's glorious there in June and July. Perhaps you'll come with me and be introduced to Jonnie.'

She coloured and said:

'You know that's impossible. You said when you were in hospital, that as soon as you got back you'd give me grounds for divorce.'

He did not look at her. He was twirling the stem of his glass round and round in his fingers. And a sudden dogged determination entered him . . . a determination never to give her grounds while Auburn Lyell was in the

161

running. Never to set her free if it was to hand her over to that cur. No! Not if Peta fought him and hated him for the rest of his life would he make it easy for her to leave him for Lyell.

His silence troubled Peta. He was being a little queer about everything, she thought. And now her resentment against him for what he had insinuated about Auburn returned. She wanted to know what it all implied and what he knew against her lover. Yet she hesitated to reopen such an unpleasant subject. She had enjoyed her meal. She had to admit that Frensham was a most interesting companion, and there had been a charm and dignity about this meal which she could not deny. A dignity in keeping with the rest of the house. Neither could she deny that had there been no Auburn, she might have been very proud to find herself the wife of such a man as Noel Frensham, and mistress of such a home.

She wished, rather wretchedly, that all the unpleasantness was over, that the divorce was over and that she and Auburn were away together in some lovely, lonely spot.

With depression weighing down upon her, she also wished beyond anything that she could see Auburn—tonight! That he could be here to tell Noel Frensham how much he loved her, and that he meant to marry her as soon as she was free.

When the meal ended and they rose to go into the library for coffee, Noel said:

'It's been a lovely birthday dinner and thank you, my dear.'

'I hope you feel all right,' she said politely.

'Much better than when I first arrived.'

'Would you—' she began.

A maid interrupted her, meeting them at the door.

'A gentleman to speak to madam on the phone. He didn't give his name.'

'For me?' asked Peta. 'Or for the doctor?'

'He asked for Mrs. Frensham, madam.'

Noel's heart seemed to leap at the sound of that name. Mrs. Frensham. Yes, by God, she was Mrs. Frensham, and his wife, and as such he had the right to take care of her

He knew perfectly well that it was Auburn Lyell phoning her. She answered the call in the library. She left the door open so that he could not help hearing what she said. And what the fellow said, his end, Noel could imagine.

'Marvellous of you to call me up, darling,' came Peta's voice, such a warm, throbbing voice that it made Noel clench his teeth . . . 'No . . . I can't possibly. No, I must stay here . . . don't be ridiculous, darling, you know I adore you, but I can't . . . what. Oh, well, perhaps then . . . I'll see. Well, if you insist . . . yes, I do want to see you terribly about a lot of things. Oh, very well, I'll come. Till then, darling . . .'

Noel, with a wooden expression, walked into the library, carefully clipping a cigar.

'That was Lyell.'

Peta turned and faced him, her dark curly-head tilted.

'Yes, it was.'

'Are you going out?'

'Later.'

'Where?'

'He said he'd call for me here in his car.'

'Not very tactful, considering it's your husband's first night home.'

'Don't be absurd. You're not really my husband, and you're going to bed early. Why shouldn't I go out?'

'As far as the law is concerned, I'm very much your husband, my dear child.'

'What are you driving at?' demanded Peta. 'There was none of this sort of talk between us in Port Said. You're assuming a sort of . . . possession of me and it doesn't exist.'

'You may be free one day, Peta, but until you are, you're not going out with Auburn Lyell.'

Her heart gave a queer twist and she stared at Noel open-mouthed, big-eyed.

'But I've never heard such utter rot. I can do as I like.'

He sat down on the arm of a leather chair and lit his cigar with a coolness which he was not exactly feeling.

'My dear Peta, presuming that you *were* going to divorce me, it would scarcely do for you to get yourself mixed up with some man. It would then look like a case of collusion.'

'I don't have to stop seeing Auburn just now and then, surely?'

Frensham looked at his wrist watch.

'Where's he taking you at this time? To a show?'

'I—I don't know.'

'I do. He's coming for you in his car, hoping to drive you to some nice quiet spot where he can make love to you.'

Peta's cheeks blazed and her eyes blazed too.

'This is beyond a joke!' she said indignantly. 'I shall do exactly what I like and go out with Burn if I like, and you shan't stop me.'

'I shall stop you, Peta. Or at least I shall try to. If it had been any other fellow—a decent fellow whom I know would make you happy—I wouldn't be doing this. I'd be keeping my word to set you free. But—'

'But *aren't* you setting me free?' she interrupted, gasping.

He put the cigar between his teeth.

'No, I don't think I am,' he said.

For a moment she could scarcely credit her hearing. Her heart seemed to leap, then sink, sink. Her very ears tingled. She sat down in a chair weakly, staring at Noel.

'You can't mean that. You can't,' she stammered.

He took the cigar from his mouth.

'Listen, Peta, I didn't want to have this all out tonight. But since you've chosen to go out with Lyell, you leave me no choice. I've got to try to put things straight.'

A servant came in with coffee and put it on a table before her. Frensham said:

'Oh, Parker, a Mr. Lyell is calling at—what time was it, darling?' He turned to Peta who, flabbergasted both at the 'darling' and the whole turn of events, told him ten o'clock. 'At ten o'clock,' Frensham said to the maid. 'Show him straight in here, will you?'

'Yes, sir.'

When they were alone again, Peta broke out:

'Have we got to have a scene tonight?'

'I hope not. I loathe scenes. I just want a quiet talk with Mr. Lyell.'

Peta clenched her hands. Her eyes were luminous with tears of sheer anger.

'Auburn will tell you what he thinks of you for this. I presume you'll let him know that you've broken your word like a—a—' She broke off stammering with rage.

'Don't bother to call me names, Peta, my dear,' Noel said quietly. 'Pour me out some coffee, there's a good child.'

'You can't treat me like this!' she said wildly. 'You can't! You promised you'd let me divorce you.'

'I've changed my mind because I don't think Auburn Lyell is fit to breathe the same air with you.'

'Stop implying things. Why not tell me

166

facts?'

'There wouldn't be time for me to tell you all the facts about Auburn Lyell before he turns up, my dear. But if you wish, I'm quite willing to tell you the story I know best. The one I was most connected with.'

The colour faded from her cheeks. She pulled herself together sufficiently to pour out the coffee. She was trembling. It was a hateful, distressing scene. For all of them. She said:

'Why couldn't you have let me see Auburn in peace? You meant to go to bed. That's why I said I'd meet him. You ought to go to bed. You're not well yet.'

'Thanks, I'm a bit tired, but I'm perfectly able to cope with things, and since Lyell has chosen to come to my house tonight to fetch you, I'll see him. The sooner we get things clear between us all the better.'

He drank his coffee, but Peta did not touch hers.

'You don't really mean, Noel, that you won't set me free?'

'I'm not going to allow you to divorce me, Peta. I have no intention of going through such unpleasantness, nor of ruining my reputation, just in order to let you go to Lyell.'

'But you got me into this mix-up—I mean, I married you because I—'

'Don't let delicacy prevent you from saying it, my poor dear,' he broke in with a shadow of a smile. 'You married me because you thought

167

I was dying. Quite so. So did I. And I seem to have created a hell of a lot of trouble by living, not only for you but for myself.'

Peta choked, drew a handkerchief from her bag and put it to her lips.

'Oh, it's all *hateful*. I didn't want you to die, you know that.'

He puffed at his cigar.

'I know that. And I know so many kind and gentle things about you, my child. That's why I want you to be happy.'

'*You* want *me* to be happy! Yet you tell me you don't intend to set me free.'

'I might divorce you,' he said coolly.

She caught her breath.

'Oh, so that's it. You don't want the divorce to be on your side. You want to put me through the mud.'

'Very aptly described—any woman going off with Lyell would go through a whole lot of mud.'

'You'll drive me crazy if you keep saying these things,' she said, shivering from head to foot. 'But I don't care! Even if I do have to go away with Auburn and you divorce me, I don't care. I love him and I'm going to him.'

'He may not take you, Peta.'

'Wait and see what he says.'

He looked at the grey ash that was beginning to form at the end of his cigar. He was so desperately tired and so reluctant to carry on with this discussion. But he had to brace himself up to it and for more to follow, once Lyell arrived. He was gambling a bit and he knew it—gambling on the fact that Lyell wouldn't allow himself to be made a co-respondent in order to take away a girl who hadn't a bean to bless herself with. Of course he might be wrong. Auburn might be genuinely in love with Peta, and then—well, then he'd have to sit back and grin and bear it. If Lyell married her, he couldn't prevent it and it would be her funeral. But what he did intend to try to prevent was a repetition of the Toni Maitland episode. And so many other episodes in Lyell's life.

He said:

'Very well, Peta. We'll wait and see what Auburn Lyell says about this divorce business.'

'It's all so mean of you!' she flashed.

'Not as mean as it seems. Shall I tell you about the case that came into my hands in my Nursing Home a couple of years ago?'

'What case?'

'Just of a girl who died . . . because of Auburn Lyell.'

Peta went white, then gave a nervous laugh.

'That sounds very melodramatic. Go on. Tell me.'

He settled himself in a chair and leaned back against the cushions and shut his eyes. And irrelevantly he said:

'I wonder if by now my birthday candles have burnt out.'

169

She did not answer.

'And if all your friendliness for me has burnt out with them. Has it, Peta?'

'You make it difficult for me,' she said. 'Because you know that I admire you, like you, and that I'm grateful for everything you've done for me. But to do *this* . . . to go back on your word . . . how can you expect . . .?'

He interrupted her.

'Let me tell you the story of Toni Maitland,' he said abruptly.

She shrugged her shoulders, sat back in her own chair, lit a cigarette, and waited for him to speak.

CHAPTER TWELVE

For a long while after Noel Frensham finished the story of Toni Maitland, Peta sat very still staring at him. She felt slightly sick and unable to move. Just one or two of the things that Noel had told her in that quiet, measured voice, stood out clearly in her brain, and she experienced so many different emotions that she would have found it impossible to state them all in words. From curiosity she changed to astonishment and from astonishment to horror and disgust . . . contempt of any man who could do such a thing to any girl. Then almost immediately from the disgust, the reactionary sensation of incredulity and remorse that she should believe, even for a single instant, one word that Noel was saying about Auburn.

It was that final emotion which she was at length able to express. She leapt to her feet, white faced and furious and cried passionately:

'It isn't true! It isn't true!'

Frensham looked up at her.

'I knew you'd say that. But it *is* true, Peta, and you must try to believe me, no matter how much you hate the truth.'

'The girl must have been neurotic . . . an erotic type . . . there are hundreds of women like that who chase men and then blame them . . .' She broke off, choking.

Noel shook his head at her. He felt intensely sorry for her. She was so young, so grand, standing there ready to defend her lover with all the strength of her ardent nature. It was her trust in Lyell which Noel found tragic and touching.

'My dear,' he said, 'you must remember that Miss Maitland was a patient of mine and that I learned a great deal about her. She was foolish, over-trusting, like yourself, and—over-generous. But she was neither neurotic nor in any way oversexed. Lyell let her down— damnably. He's let others down. I could tell you a dozen stories that I've heard. He has that reputation.'

For the fraction of a second only Peta

wavered, then broke out again:

'It's all rot! Just because he's so frightfully good-looking and attractive, people talk about him . . . possibly other men are jealous of his conquests. And women turn round and blame him after they've thrown themselves at his head and he doesn't want them.'

'Peta, Peta! That's not the case.'

'Well, it's what I believe. I know him. I love him and I trust him.'

Noel stood up. He put the stump of his cigar into a tray. He felt so very tired.

Peta added:

'I shall ask Burn about this Maitland girl and tell him the other things you said.'

Noel felt slightly exasperated.

'My dear child, obviously he'll deny these stories. He wouldn't be likely to admit the truth of them.'

'You make him out to be something vile!'

'Maybe that's what I devoutly believe,' was Noel's grim response.

'Then I think you're hateful,' said Peta, her cheeks and her eyes blazing. 'And you're a cad to refuse a divorce that you promised me.'

Noel made a gesture of despair.

'Very well. Think of me as a cad. It isn't an epithet I have had hurled at me by anybody else, as far as I know.'

She bit her lip, her breast rising and falling in her agitation.

'No, I don't quite understand *why* you have

172

changed so completely. I thought you *were*—frightfully decent. I know you must be, really, because everybody says so, and . . .' She stammered and paused, feeling utterly confused.

Frensham came close to her and put a hand on her shoulder. He felt a great tenderness for her.

'I understand so completely what you're thinking, Peta. And naturally you must think of me as you find me. It may seem to you that I'm being caddish and mean to break my word, but I cannot and will not make this divorce easy for you if Auburn Lyell is the man you want to marry.'

She wrenched her shoulder away from his touch. His very kindness and gentleness infuriated her.

'You have no right to say who I am or am not to marry. Oh, I was certainly off my head when I married you. I might have known something like this would happen.'

He turned from her and picked up his cigar again.

'We shan't get any further talking this way! I've told you a horrifying story, but you don't believe it and it hasn't impressed you. You take it for granted that what I say is wrong, and everything that Lyell tells you is like the gospel. That means we shall only talk in circles, so let's stop it and wait until Lyell comes. By all means tell him what I've said—ask him if he wishes to be cited as a co-respondent so that he can marry you, and then see . . .'

Peta felt sick again. She threw a nervous glance at Noel's back. He was so very quiet and determined and seemed so sure of himself. She thought how horrible it would be if he was right and she was making a mistake about Auburn. But hot on the track of doubt came that burning loyalty which Peta always felt for those that she loved and could not help but feel for the man who had so completely taken possession of her heart.

It wasn't true, it couldn't be . . . and she was going to take Auburn's word. She said, more calmly:

'I don't see how you can want to keep me as your wife. It doesn't mean any more to you than it does to me . . . this sort of farce of living together.'

He did not turn to her. He did not want her to see what lay in his eyes. But he would like to have told her then how very much it did mean to him to have her in this house and what a lot he would give for the chance to win her love and her trust as Auburn Lyell had won them.

It was a pretty tangle! A grim position for them both to be in. He might well echo her wish that they had never married. He had been happier as he was . . . his interest centred solely in his medical work . . . the Noel who was entirely and absolutely the doctor . . . the man whose imagination no woman had captured.

174

During the half-hour which they waited for Auburn to come, there was a tense, uncomfortable silence between them. Noel, looking as grim as he felt, picked up an evening paper and pretended to read it, and Peta walked nervously round the library, looking at a book here and there, distracted by thoughts of her lover, of her present position, and of what the meeting between the two men would bring forth.

When at length she heard a car drive up to the house, a door slam and the front door-bell ring, she was in a bad state of nerves. She came up to Frensham and looked at him, her face flushed and mutinous.

'That's Auburn . . . now we'll see . . . we'll see how wrong you are . . .'

For a moment Noel gripped her hand and held on to it hard.

'Try to face this without too much prejudice, Peta, I implore you.'

She drew her hand away without answering. The library door opened and Auburn Lyell walked in.

'Peta—' he began.

Then he saw the man who was standing with his back to the mantelpiece, and stopped. He had expected Peta to be alone. It never entered his head that he would be called upon tonight to face the doctor whom she had married. He looked quickly from Frensham to Peta, and saw at once that something was

175

wrong. She was white and trembling.

She came towards him and said:

'Dr. Frensham insists upon seeing you. I think it's just as well we should all get this business quite clear. Dr. Frensham seems to have a mistaken idea about you and your attitude towards me, Burn. I'm sorry to drag you into any unpleasantness, but I hope you won't mind . . .'

Auburn lifted his brows. His handsome face was expressionless. But, to himself, he said:

'*Hell!*'

'You'd better come and sit down, Lyell,' said Frensham in his quiet, modulated voice.

The eyes of the two men met. And Auburn Lyell saw that here he had no weakling to deal with. Peta's 'husband' was a man of resolution. And there was no uncertain enmity written across that thin, tired face of his.

Frensham told himself that Auburn Lyell was certainly good-looking enough to attract any woman. It was the first time he had seen Toni Maitland's seducer. A fine, debonair figure of a man, Lyell—a little too perfectly dressed, perhaps—an affectation, that evening suit which was dark mulberry colour instead of black. He was altogether a little too sleek . . . but marvellously good-looking with his fair shining head and blue, insolent eyes with their sculptured lids. Curious, Frensham thought, that a body which had been given such faultless grace should contain so mean, so

176

graceless a soul.

'What's all this about?' murmured Lyell, and did not sit in the chair that Frensham indicated, but with an air of nonchalance smiled at Peta, took a cigarette from his case and lit it. 'I didn't think I was to have the pleasure of meeting er—Dr. Frensham.'

'I don't think there's going to be much pleasure about it,' said Peta dryly. 'You might as well know straight away, Burn, that Noel has changed his mind and isn't going to give me that divorce.'

Lyell looked at the elder man with guileless surprise.

'Aren't you? But, good God, sir, I thought it was taken for granted that you'd set Peta free. You told her so in Port Said. You rather owe it to her, don't you? I mean, it's a damned awkward position, and all that . . . the deathbed business not turning out as you all expected . . . but if a woman marries a man out of kindness . . . damn it all . . . it's up to him to put things right, isn't it?'

Before Noel could reply Peta broke out:

'I did only marry him because he persuaded me. Nobody need think that I was after his money. I agreed that it would be very pleasant to inherit what he had to leave, but it was never the money I wanted. And Noel knows that.'

'I have never disputed that,' said Noel. 'I'm perfectly well aware that you haven't a

177

grasping or mercenary nature, Peta.'

'And I've told him, Burn,' added Peta, 'that I wouldn't touch any money of his, not a penny, even if I was allowed to divorce him and could legally claim a third of his income. I know you agree with me, don't you? You wouldn't want me to take his money.'

Auburn flicked the ash from his cigarette. He did not look at Peta, nor at Frensham, who was watching him between narrowed lids. His thoughts were far from being agreeable ones. He was recalling a very distressing morning in the city . . . a morning spent with his father, looking over the newly audited books of the firm. They had had to realise what a frightful crash they'd come to during these last few months. And then, he had a few thousand pounds' worth of personal bills waiting to be paid. He could carry on for the moment, but he knew that the day must come when, unless business took a miraculous turn for the better, his creditors would realise the situation and become pressing.

He had expected that Peta would get a nice little sum of money out of the divorce from Frensham . . . a third of what must be a considerable income. God! he thought, it was scarcely the time for him to contemplate marrying a girl without a bean. How damned awkward! And he was so much in love with the girl, too. Intolerable of this fellow to change his mind. Why had he done it? He supposed

178

he would find out in a moment, and meanwhile he must not show what lay in his mind if he wanted all that this adorable Peta had to offer a man.

He put out a hand to her. Immediately she clung to it, her heart warming. She whispered:

'Tell him what you feel about me, Burn. Tell him that you love me.'

'But that goes without saying,' drawled Auburn. 'I'm terribly in love with you, my sweet, but I really don't see why I should make a declaration of my feelings just to impress Dr. Frensham.'

Noel had always hated the thought of this man, and now that he saw him he loathed him as he would a crawling slug. He was psychologist enough to be able to read the fellow through and through. He knew that he wasn't genuine—he never had been genuine and never could be.

'Look here, Lyell,' said Noel, 'I'll need more than a verbal declaration of your feelings to induce me to believe that you are really fond of Peta, and that you intend to marry her.'

'What the devil do you mean?' asked Lyell.

Peta's small fingers clutched Auburn's, spasmodically.

'Burn, he's been saying things like this the whole evening . . . ever since he got back. He's told me stories about you . . . he wants me to believe that you're incapable of sincerity and that you've made a whole lot of promises to

179

other women which you've never kept. And he says he knows so much about you that he won't allow me to divorce him in order to marry you. I can't get my freedom unless he divorces *me*. He says I must go away with you.'

An instant's silence. And again Auburn's thoughts were by no means pleasant ones. He felt immensely chagrined by the turn events had taken. Here was a pretty *dénouement*. He could see now how the land lay. Frensham knew all about Toni, of course. Perhaps he knew other things as well. So he was going to make it as hard as he could for Peta to get her freedom.

'Burn,' came Peta's passionate young voice, 'it wouldn't matter to you, would it? If it has to be that way . . . you won't mind if I don't, will you? Tell me. Tell *him*! He doesn't believe in your love for me.'

Auburn cleared his throat. He would have to go very carefully if he wanted to keep Peta. He would have to give up the idea of marrying her under the present awkward financial conditions, but given time he might eventually win her without getting himself into difficulties. Yes, to temporise was the thing. So he stood up, put an arm round Peta's shoulders, and assumed an expression of outraged dignity.

'This is damned ridiculous. Why shouldn't he believe that I love you?'

'Because,' cut in Frensham, 'I know too

much about you.'

His voice was cold as ice. Not that he was feeling cold. He experienced the hottest sensation of jealousy at the sight of Peta's slim young figure in the circle of Auburn Lyell's arm. He loathed the thought of the fellow touching her . . . hated to see the way she leaned against him, confiding, trusting, adoring him. Noel was horrified at the poignancy of his own feelings. He wanted to smash his fist in the fellow's handsome, hypocritical face.

'And what *does* Dr. Frensham know about me?' drawled Auburn.

'He's told me a story,' said Peta, 'about a girl named Toni Maitland. He says she was a patient of his and that you drove her to suicide.'

Auburn did not even change colour. He said:

'That sounds very dramatic. And isn't it rather a serious allegation, Dr. Frensham?'

'Do you deny it?'

'Absolutely.'

Peta's spirits rose sky-high. She put an arm through Auburn's, pressed it to her side, and flung Noel a defiant look.

'There you are!'

Noel felt almost angry with her.

'Did you expect him to admit it?'

'What exactly have you told Peta about this girl, Toni Maitland?' asked Auburn.

'The whole story as I know it—and as Miss

181

Maitland told it to me before she died.'

Auburn passed a tongue over his lips.

'Perhaps you haven't explained to Peta that Toni Maitland was a very unbalanced kind of girl—in fact, I might almost say she was a borderline case. Just because I was idiot enough to flirt with her she took me seriously and made my life hell, following me around, then tried to blame it on me because she lost her job and became down and out. She was nothing but an exhibitionist. No doubt she told you a very ugly story, but there wasn't necessarily a grain of truth in it.'

Frensham clenched his hands.

'That's a lie, and you know it. Toni Maitland was quite sane and no exhibitionist. She was just a child who took your word and gave everything she had to you, then when you were tired of her . . .' He broke off, breathing quickly.

Peta said:

'It's no use going over that. Burn says it isn't true and I believe him.'

Frensham swung round to her.

'Don't take my word, then. Go and ask the nurses who were with her at the end. Go and ask her friend who shared the flat with her and who brought her to me. What was her name . . . Betty Phillips, that was it . . . do *you* remember Betty Phillips, Lyell? I don't think you'd care to face her in front of Peta and ask her whether that poor child Toni was out of her

182

mind . . . until you nearly sent her out of it by your callous, inhuman behaviour.'

The colour was mounting to Auburn's forehead now. Little drops of sweat glistened on his temples. It was not very pleasant having the ghost of Toni dragged into the light like this. It was of his many 'affairs' the one which he least liked to remember. Just now and again . . . when he had had a little too much to drink . . . when he was alone . . . he was haunted by the picture of Toni as he had last seen her on the night on which he had finally left her. Toni, on the floor at his feet, clawing wildly at his knees, lifting a desperate face, besmudged with tears, with agony . . . Toni sobbing horribly, saying in between the sobs:

'Don't leave me . . . don't walk out on me, Auburn darling. If you do I shall kill myself. Auburn, I'm so frightened. I think I'm going to have a baby, Auburn. You can't leave me like that. Auburn, I shall *die*.'

And he had gone without caring. And she had died.

Singularly unpleasant recollections for a man. Damned annoying that it should have been the specialist who attended Toni, of all men in the world, to marry Peta.

Auburn wanted Peta, with her enchanting touches of prudery, blent with passion . . . Peta, who would be so sweet, to love . . . to initiate into the art of loving as he knew it.

'Well, would you care to face Miss Phillips

183

in front of Peta?' repeated Noel. 'Shall I try to find her for you?'

'You're taking rather too much on yourself,' said Auburn. 'You may have married Peta, but she doesn't in any way belong to you, and I'll trouble you to remember it.'

'Quite so,' seconded Peta. 'And he can bring anybody he likes to tell me things, but I shan't believe them. I shall believe you, Burn.'

'Oh, God!' Frensham said under his breath.

Auburn took heart at Peta's words. She was a grand little champion, he thought, and so much more attractive than one of these suspicious, jealous women who might have 'put him on the spot' by demanding to see Betty Phillips and a few other witnesses of the Maitland affair. He felt grateful to her, quite truly fond of her tonight. He drew her closer to his side.

'My sweet, your faith is wonderful, and you won't regret giving it to me.'

'I know that,' she whispered.

For an instant her gaze rested upon him tenderly. Then she turned to Noel. His face gave her almost a shock. It was so white and so strained—his lips puckered as though he were in pain. And suddenly her anger against him evaporated. Auburn loved her and she loved him and trusted in him. They had got the better of poor old Noel. How ill he looked! Quite kindly she said:

'Look here, Noel, it's no use bringing up

184

past episodes about Auburn. I daresay he's had his fling like lots of other men, but it's not going to alter my feeling for him. Why upset yourself—all of us—by this sort of scene?'

He looked at her in silence for a moment. He was conscious of such fatigue that he could scarcely think. But jealousy was still gnawing at him, jealousy and the intense wish to save Peta from herself . . . and from this man.

'Very well,' he said. 'If Lyell denies everything and you choose to take his word and refuse to see anybody else who knows the truth about Miss Maitland, I can do no more.'

'You've done too much already,' said Auburn.

Frensham looked him in the eyes.

'Do you intend to marry Peta?'

'Certainly.'

'Then you don't mind if I file a petition, and cite you?'

'I think,' said Auburn, 'that you might reserve some of the names you have called me for yourself, if that's how you mean to behave to Peta. Why do you want to put her in the wrong?'

'Why should I sully my own reputation in order to hand her over to a man like yourself, Lyell?'

'I won't be insulted by you, Dr. Frensham. I'll have you in the Courts for libel before you've finished.'

Frensham gave a faint, cold smile.

'I don't think you'd dare do that. You couldn't afford to have too much dragged to the light.'

Peta looked from one man to the other, her heart thumping, her cheeks changing from red to white and from white to red again.

'Must we go on with this . . . this beastly conversation?'

'Yes, we must,' said Noel. 'And I repeat my question to Mr. Lyell. Does he mind if I file a petition and cite him for the divorce?'

Auburn moved uneasily.

'You can't do that to Peta,' he parried. 'You promised to let her divorce you.'

'I've changed my mind and I shan't change it again. If Peta wants her freedom she'll have to prove to herself exactly how willing you are to go through divorce and marriage for her sake.'

Auburn cleared his throat and glanced at Peta, whose large brown eyes questioned him. He felt rather cornered. And there was no man on the face of the earth whom he disliked so intensely as Dr. Noel Frensham. He said:

'You may want to drag her into the limelight and ruin her reputation, but I don't.'

Ah!' said Noel with narrowed eyes. 'So you're trying to wriggle out of it. You *don't* want this divorce.'

'Naturally I want it, but I don't see why she should be made to pay for the mistake she made in marrying a dying man who didn't die, and had no damned right to persuade her into such folly.'

Noel felt all fatigue lifted from him. His brain grew alert again. He had a sudden stimulating feeling that Auburn Lyell was going to behave just as he expected him to behave. That he wasn't going to come out of this scene as well as Peta wanted him to. To show Peta what Lyell really was . . . to show him up . . . that was all that Noel wanted. To see her chuck Lyell out of her life. And then, later, if she still wanted her freedom, how gladly he would give it to her.

'I admit,' he said, 'that I was responsible for the marriage and that Peta made a mistake since I unfortunately lived. But that doesn't alter *your* feeling for her. If you want her you'll help her get her freedom and stand by her.'

Auburn looked down at the girl who was still close to his side, one slim shaking hand locked in his.

'Do you think it fair on yourself that you should be dragged through the Courts as a divorcée? My God, darling, you're so good, so absolutely good through and through . . . I wouldn't want that to happen to you.'

Peta was completely blinded by that speech. It seemed to her that Noel was ready to sling the mud and Auburn anxious to protect her from it. She said:

'It's sweet of you to think of me and naturally I don't want to be divorced, but

187

anything to be free . . . and to be able to marry you.'

'Well,' came from Frensham, 'do I file my petition, Lyell?'

He jerked at his collar.

'You can hardly do that until we give you grounds for the divorce. There are none at the moment.'

Frensham gave his slow, cold smile and a half bow.

'As you wish. So I shall not file the petition until you give me the grounds. And meanwhile . . . Peta remains my wife.'

Peta drew away from Auburn. She both looked and felt bewildered now. Auburn was lighting a fresh cigarette. She could not see his face, could not see that it was dark with rage. She felt that in some mysterious way, in spite of Auburn's protests of love and denials of the accusations levelled against him, Noel had gained a point and she did not quite know how it had happened. Then Frensham said:

'If you'll forgive me, I'll leave you. I'm dead tired and I think it's time I turned in.'

Neither Peta nor Auburn answered him. He gave Peta a look of great tenderness and melancholy, then turned and walked out of the library, leaving them alone. And as he went he thought:

'God knows what will come of this. And God knows what he'll say and do now. But for the moment, she stays with me.'

188

That thought was the only thing to console Noel Frensham on the first night home as he went up the big staircase and to his bedroom. That and the belief which he had in Peta . . . a belief that in spite of her blind adoration of Auburn she would not surrender easily . . . and would not give him those grounds for the divorce until she was sufficiently convinced of Auburn's sincerity, to go away with him and never come back.

He was gambling on her strength of character and her fair-minded, decent attitude towards life. Well—if he lost, life would not have much meaning for him, because he loved her as he had never before loved anybody and in all probability would never love again.

CHAPTER THIRTEEN

As soon as the library door had closed upon Noel, Peta found herself in her lover's arms. For a few moments all that she had meant to say went out of her head. He was holding her so intoxicatingly close . . . and his lips were so hot and urgent upon her mouth . . . how could she think sanely or speak anything that was in her mind? He was telling her that he adored her; that she was the loveliest, sweetest thing in the world.

At length he drew her to the deep

189

cushioned sofa at right angles to the fireplace and sat there with her, gathered close in his embrace. His slim magnetic fingers wandered through her curls, caressed her cheeks and throat. He said:

'I love you . . . I love you. I've been crazy to kiss you like this . . . all day . . . God! it was awful to come and fetch you and find you with that damned doctor. Why did you ever marry him? You belong to me . . . to me . . .'

Her hand smoothed the glistening fairness of his head and stroked his cheek. Breathless from his kisses, she could only shake her head at him mutely. And then he kissed her eyes and told her that she had the longest and most alluring lashes that he had ever seen.

'They're like a little girl's,' he said. 'You are just a little girl. Mine. Tell me you're mine.'

She whispered:

'You know. You know!'

His lips claimed hers again. And then something made her draw back. That *something* which she never quite understood but which always came to her rescue. Some deep reservation and pride which kept her mistress of herself even in the most devastating moments when she was in Auburn's arms.

'Darling, please . . .'

'Don't you love me?' he said. 'Are you afraid of me?'

'Perhaps, a little . . .' She laughed shakily. '. . . And a great deal more of myself.'

He lifted her wrist and kissed it, dropped swift, warm kisses into the palm of her hand, and finally came to the wedding-ring on her finger. With an angry movement, he pulled it off.

'Damn and blast that thing and the whole outlandish marriage.'

She was conscious of no particular feeling about the ring, but she took it back from Auburn and replaced it on her finger. And now she drew away from him and grew calm again and thoughtful.

'Yes, it's shattering. But I did it and there you are. We've got to talk things over, Auburn, That's why I want to be sane.'

It was the last thing he wanted her to be, but he let her have her way.

'I can't say I'm very impressed by your doctor. He's an impossible cad to have broken his word to you like this.'

Her brows drew together.

'He isn't really a cad. He's just not himself about this business. I would never have believed it of him.'

'So you're defending him!'

'No, but I want to be fair. I know that Noel Frensham isn't . . . couldn't be described as a "cad".'

'Did you like the things he had to say about me?'

'You know I didn't, and I didn't believe them. He seems to have been biased because he was this . . . this Maitland girl's doctor, and I suppose he credited all that she had to say.'

'Well, as long as you don't, nothing matters.'

'Of course I don't.'

'You still love me in spite of the fact that Frensham's so prejudiced against me?'

'Of course, darling. What he says doesn't matter. I use my own judgment,' said Peta, tilting her dark young head with a proud movement.

'You're very adorable,' he said, and wished gloomily that she had some money of her own, and had not been a penniless nursery-governess before she married Frensham.

'But what about this divorce?' she continued. 'That's what worries me. That's what's so mean of Noel. No matter what his prejudices are, he had no right to make it difficult for me to get free. Only I want you to know that I am willing to go through anything in order to be with you . . . anything.' She repeated the word and gave him a quick, shy look which would have put any man but Auburn Lyell to shame.

He merely drew her into his arms again.

'Angel! You're too sweet to me. But I can't drag you through the divorce courts. How can I?'

'We must if I want to be free.'

'Perhaps you could persuade Frensham to change his mind.'

She knit her brows.

'I don't want to be beholden to him for anything if he's your enemy.'

'But you owe it to yourself, darling. Mud clings, and even when we were married there would be certain people who would remember the position . . . you would be cut by some . . . misjudged by others . . . it wouldn't be fair to you. Frensham obviously hasn't got your interests at heart. He's only thinking of himself and his own reputation, but I'm thinking of *you*.'

She felt confused and unhappy. With an exasperated sigh she said:

'I honestly don't think he is like that. It's just that he seems to hate you.'

'I'll lay you a bet that it's because he wants you for himself,' said Auburn with a little sneer on his curved, sensual mouth. 'Yes, I honestly believe that fellow is doing and saying all these things because he wants you for himself.'

Peta crimsoned.

'I don't think so. Anyhow, I've *got* to be free.'

'Naturally, darling, and I want you to be. I want to marry you as soon as you are.'

She gave him a warm, sweet look.

'Darling Burn! Then it looks as though we'll have to put ourselves in the wrong.'

He was silent a moment. Then he said:

'Frensham's going to come out of this on top, but it will sink you—and me. I, although not a doctor, have a business and my own good reputation is valuable, added to which it would break my mother's heart. She's an old lady and not strong, and I'm her only son—the only child. I've told you before that I've got a couple of old-fashioned parents, and the idea of me running away with a married woman would kill them.'

Peta drew away from him. She felt the sudden need for a cigarette and lit one with none too steady a hand. Through the tall open windows of the library the night blew cooler after the day's warmth. The library seemed to be growing cold and Peta in her chiffon dress shivered.

She was very tired by now. From the moment that Noel had got back in this house tonight, she had been tossed on a sea of emotions. Her nerves were frayed. And her brain would not think straight for her. Things were not working out as she had anticipated. She had felt so sure that Auburn would agree to anything, everything so as to win her. But of course, she told herself, she mustn't be unreasonable. It was quite just, what he said, about having his own business reputation to consider, and his parents.

He was repeating now that he was thinking mainly of her. It was grossly unfair that she should be put in the wrong just because Frensham didn't like her choice of a man. Surely she could make Frensham see that and eventually persuade him to change his mind.

He continued to argue and protest on her behalf until there was no doubt left in her mind that Auburn loved her, and that nothing that he said sprang from any desire to quit. Indeed, Auburn assured her that should she fail to make Noel change his mind, he would, of course, take her away. His reputation and his parents would have to 'go hang'.

Then Peta said, miserably:

'It all seems such a frightful mess and all my fault for consenting to that marriage in Port Said. Perhaps you'd better give me up, Auburn. I don't want to be the cause of hurting you or your people.'

He smothered her with kisses and fresh protestations of his love.

'Don't dare say anything so foolish. I shall never give you up. But why should we give in to Frensham right at the beginning and let him get away with things just because he hates me? I tell you he's only damn jealous, but when you've made him see that you intend to have your freedom at any price, he'll give in. Anyhow, whatever happens, you'll find me waiting, darling. I adore you. I always will.'

She put an arm round his neck and for a moment looked up into his face, her eyes filled with tears.

'Oh, Burn, you do mean that? There isn't a grain of truth in what he says about this other girl . . . about other women . . .'

'Not a grain of truth,' he whispered. 'As I've

always told you, I've had my affairs, but I've always played the game.'

'I believe you,' she said, and her lips quivered into a smile. He took out a silk handkerchief and wiped away her tears.

'And you agree, my sweet, that we'd be foolish to give in to Frensham at once . . . that we might try to get your freedom with the least possible damage to yourself? After all, I've too much respect for you to rush you away and just let him file a petition. If I did, it would show I did not care what I did to hurt you.'

Those words redoubled her faith in him.

'You're grand, Burn darling.'

He felt rather grand. He even began to think that he was behaving a lot better than Noel Frensham. But at the back of his mind he was working out a scheme for inducing Peta to accompany him on his next trip to Paris . . . without turning himself into the co-respondent of any divorce case in which he would have to pay all the costs and damages.

Peta, leaning back in the curve of her lover's arm, growing suddenly drowsy and happy, thought things over and decided that Auburn was right. Why *should* Noel make her pay for their marriage just because he did not like the man of her choice? She would try to make him see reason. She would not be bullied into leaving the house and ruining both her reputation and Auburn's just to satisfy Noel Frensham. Perhaps it was selfish of her. But the other thing would be selfish of him. It didn't always pay to give in.

Like so many soft-hearted, romantic people, Peta possessed a dogged determination when her back was to the wall. She could be hard when she chose. Under Auburn's influence that hardness came to light and was directed against Noel.

When Auburn left her that evening she was fully determined to fight it out with Noel. And she emerged from the chaos of events that evening triumphantly sure of Auburn and herself.

On her way up to bed she walked into the boudoir and switched on the lights.

The ardent glow which was still upon her, coming straight from Auburn's good-night kiss, suddenly faded and her lips took a serious curve. She was looking at the candles over the fireplace. They had gutted and burnt out, and there was nothing left but the grease dripping down the gilt sticks. There is nothing more melancholy than the sight of a burnt-out candle. And Peta was forced to remember the significance of these two. She had lit them, just as Noel's mother used to do, in celebration of Noel's birthday. What a birthday it had been for the poor man! What a home-coming! A disagreeable battle of words. And how ill he still looked.

She began to feel sorry for him, a little remorseful for her hardness. After all, she would not be showing an attractive attitude by making him feel it was better that he should have died out there in Port Said.

Standing in this room which had been Mary Frensham's, Peta suddenly felt cold and unhappy. It was almost as though the spirit of the dead mother came to reproach her for her treatment of her son. But it was his own fault, she argued to herself. He shouldn't have said such dreadful things about Auburn. That was what made her so angry and resentful. That, and his going back on his word. Of course Auburn maintained that he was jealous. Was that true? she wondered, uneasily.

While she stood there, shivering a little in her chiffon dress, her big brown eyes fixed doubtfully on the sad spectacle of the gutted candles, she heard the door open and turned to see Noel standing there. He was in pyjamas and dressing-gown—a wine-coloured silk dressing-gown with black revers, familiar to her. He had worn it on the ship and in hospital. He looked white and stern. As she turned to him he said in a voice of cold courtesy:

'I beg your pardon. I thought you'd gone to bed.'

'I—I'm just going,' she found herself stammering. For some reason or other she felt like a guilty child in his presence. Yet downstairs, with Auburn to back her up, she had felt quite the reverse, quite convinced that she was in the right.

'I remembered the candles,' he said. 'And I wondered if they were safely out.'

'They are out,' she said.

'Then good night,' he said.

She hesitated an instant. But as he turned to go, she called him back.

He turned, wearing an expression of faint surprise.

'You want me?'

'Just to say that I . . . that I'm sorry all this has happened,' she said, conscious of intense embarrassment and equally conscious that Auburn would have thought an apology, or any expression of sympathy, gratuitous and undeserved by Noel. She even thought that she was a little disloyal to Auburn by being nice to Noel, but something stronger than herself propelled the words.

Some of the severity on Frensham's face relaxed. Poor pretty child, he thought, so utterly charming in her inexperience, her indecision, and all the conflicting emotions which he knew full well must be harrowing her. He realised that it wasn't easy for her to get a sense of proportion over this thing. And it was only natural that she should defend her lover to the teeth. That was the way she was made. But he wished to God something, *someone* would tear the scales from her eyes and make her see Auburn Lyell as he really was. He said:

'It's much too late for us to stand here being

199

sorry about what's happened, my dear.'

She looked at her wrist-watch, her cheeks burning.

'Yes, it's long past midnight.'

'Go to bed,' he said kindly.

Again something that she could not explain prompted her to say:

'But I am sorry. I've taken so much from you . . . living here in this beautiful house . . . and, and other things. It seems ungrateful and mean of me to be so antagonistic, but you did say such awful things about Auburn. It made me lose my temper.'

'Naturally,' he said. 'The only thing I wish you wouldn't lose is your critical faculty. You're a sensible girl, Peta. You shouldn't wrap people up in silver paper and label them 'Perfect,' just because you love them.'

'But I don't!' she protested. 'I'm sure that Auburn has faults, and that he's been a flirt, and . . .'

'Tell me,' Noel interrupted abruptly. 'After talking things over, has he decided to take you away and marry you?'

Her colour deepened.

'Oh, I daresay you'll misunderstand him, but he thought it was grossly unfair that I should be made a divorcée, and he said he would not take me away for the present. He hoped we might all come to some other arrangement. He was only thinking of me.'

Something leapt in Noel's breast. Triumph,

200

even though the taste of it was bitter in his mouth because it could bring him no nearer to this girl. But things were working out as he had anticipated. Auburn Lyell wasn't so anxious to face this divorce.

'I suppose he wasn't thinking of himself at all? You don't for a moment believe that he would like to wriggle out of the divorce now that he knows it will bring him into the action?'

Peta's breathing quickened.

'Those are the sort of things you say which make me feel that I . . .'

'That you hate me,' Noel finished for her with a faint smile.

She turned from him, beating one small fist upon the other.

'Oh, why must you take it for granted that Auburn doesn't love me sincerely, or that he wants to back out of his promises? He's thinking of me, I tell you.'

'And I'm not, eh?'

'How can you be when you want to throw all the blame on me?'

'You're wrong. I'm doing this solely and entirely to prove to you that Auburn Lyell will never allow himself to be made a co-respondent. He hasn't the guts. And—for your private information, my child—the firm of Lyell & Son is not doing so well. There are rumours in the City that they might go bust. Do you think, if they do, that Auburn Lyell will want just a sweet romance with a girl who isn't worth a penny? No! He might like to marry the woman who has divorced me and can claim some of my money.'

'Don't go on!' broke in Peta furiously. 'I won't listen to you!'

She tried to rush past him and out of the boudoir, but he caught her wrist.

'Don't lose your temper with me again, Peta. I may provoke you, but I beg you to deal with this thing calmly and think quietly over every word that I say.'

Panting, white with resentment, Peta looked up at him with her big flashing eyes.

'We shall see what Auburn does! As for that business about money . . . that's beastly of you. I don't believe it.'

'You'll believe nothing until it's proved to you, and then I suppose it will be too late,' said Noel.

Her rage subsided. She drew away her wrist.

'Oh dear!' she sighed. 'I didn't mean there to be another row. It's all so . . . so horrible.'

'It'll work itself out,' he said. 'And meanwhile believe who you will and what you like, but I ask you to do one thing.'

'What?'

'Go on living here as my wife.'

'I'd much rather not.'

'For your own sake it's best, Peta.'

'I see no object if I'm to be divorced.'

'Wait until that position arises, Peta. Your

202

gallant Auburn isn't ready to take you away *yet*! He may . . . oh yes . . . I admit that he *may* have every intention of marrying you. But until it's finally fixed, you had much better stay here with me. I'll make no demands on you. You needn't worry about that.'

'That's not what I'm worrying about,' she said, flushing.

'Then let us see what happens,' he said. 'And at least try to believe that I'm your friend.'

She gave a short nervous laugh.

'You don't show friendship by hurling perpetual insults at the man I love.'

His face suddenly contracted.

'How well and loyally you love, Peta. Oh, I wish to God . . .'

He caught himself up, breathing heavily. He was nearer than he had ever been to catching her in his arms and beseeching her to stay with him . . . not for the moment . . . but for always. But he restrained that impulse with all the strength that was in him.

Peta, looking up into his smouldering eyes, had a sudden lightning insight into what lay in his mind. *Auburn was right.* Noel Frensham *was* in love with her. That instant's revelation left her more than ever confused. It was the most awkward and disturbing thing that could have happened, she reflected. And quite wrongfully she imagined that it was his personal feeling for her which was prompting

203

his attempt to separate her from Auburn—rather than that he really knew or believed that Auburn was a rotter. By very virtue of that mistake she softened to Noel. What romantic woman can be bitter or angry with a man who has an unrequited passion for her? It was not a question of vanity with Peta. She had no wish for any man she did not care for to fall in love with her. And she was quite truly abashed by what she had discovered—and was amazed, for it had never entered her head that Noel Frensham would ever grow to care for her that way.

While she stood there, confusedly pondering over things, Noel said:

'Is it to be a truce between us, or a battle, Peta?'

'It looks to me like a battle,' she said miserably. 'I want my freedom, and I admit that I'm selfish enough to want it with the least possible hurt to Auburn and myself. But I think that's only fair. And you think otherwise, and want to put obstacles in my path. So we're bound to fight, aren't we?'

'Very well,' he said grimly. All passion had died down in him now and he was white and stern again. 'We must fight, Peta. But meanwhile—you stay here.'

She spread out her hands with a gesture of despair. There seemed nothing else to say. But as he turned to go, the old kindly Peta said:

'You must take care of yourself, you know.

You aren't strong yet.'

'I'm very well, thanks—merely tired and unable to sleep,' he said in the same grim voice.

She played with a fold of her chiffon dress. She had never felt so miserable. The whole thing was grossly perplexing, destructive to her peace of mind and heart. She could not help liking Noel Frensham, and yet if he was to be Auburn's enemy, he must also be hers.

Frensham looked at the bent head with the dark brown curls and at the shoulders which he had thought of, on board ship, as 'rose-misted marble,' and was as miserable—if not more so—than she was.

Suddenly she lifted her head and said in her impulsive way:

'Under these circumstances how can you want me to stay here and be called "Mrs. Frensham," and perhaps have to meet your sister and friends? Wouldn't you rather I went away tomorrow?'

'No,' he said. 'If this thing is to end finally in divorce, one way or the other, let it be said that for a decent space of time, at least, you lived in my house. Good night, Peta.'

'Good night,' she said.

And they went to their separate rooms and closed their doors upon their separate griefs and perplexities. At length the big house in Wimpole Street was wrapped in silence and darkness—and sleep.

CHAPTER FOURTEEN

The next week was one of continued perplexity and not much happiness for Peta. What it was for Noel, she could only dimly guess by the strained look on his face.

From her own point of view, there was a disastrous sequel to their scene *à trois*, when Auburn telephoned her the following morning to say that he must leave town for Manchester at once, and would be away on business until the following week-end. She was bitterly disappointed because she wanted now, more than ever, to see him. But she knew that he was a busy man and, from what Noel had said, business was bad at the moment, so it was no wonder he was called away. But she felt curiously deserted. Neither did she particularly relish being left alone to cope with her position as Mrs. Noel Frensham.

Auburn, however, was so charming and regretful over the telephone, that she could not do otherwise than feel that warmth and belief in him which he always inspired.

'I'll write to you every day,' he said, 'and every minute away from you will seem hellishly long, my angel. Take care of yourself and don't let that damned doctor bully you.'

She had given a non-committal reply, because Noel was not, in effect, a bullying type. But she knew what Auburn meant.

When she told Noel that Auburn would be away a week, he said nothing, merely gave that faint cynical smile which she was beginning to know, and which induced her to flash at him childishly:

'I suppose you think he's gone away with some woman and that it isn't business at all!'

Noel, sitting in the chair before his desk in his consulting-room, smiled broadly and not cynically this time.

'What a baby you are, Peta.'

She felt that she had been silly, turned away from him with crimson cheeks and wondered how she was going to bear a whole week without her lover.

But it proved not an uneventful week. She was plunged, willy-nilly, into a sequence of unexpected duties as the wife of a man whom, she learned day by day, was one of the most eminent and sought-after consultants in London.

From the moment people knew that Dr. Frensham had returned home, there came a stream of visitors, eager to see and congratulate him on his miraculous recovery from that fell Eastern disease which had overtaken him in India. The telephone rang all day. Miss Turner, Noel's secretary, was driven almost to distraction by the innumerable calls and inquiries, until Peta offered to relieve her of some of them. And there were arrears of correspondence to be dealt with. Flowers poured in from 'grateful patients.' The house began to look like a conservatory, and Peta really saw very little of Noel, who spent a lot of his time attending to his affairs.

He needed distraction from those poignant feelings that Peta roused in him, but he was wise enough to refrain from returning to actual work, until he had a longer rest. He cancelled his intended holiday up in Scotland because he knew that Peta would not go with him, and he did not wish to leave her here alone. The crisis with Auburn Lyell had not yet come, but he was going to look after her until that day arrived, he told himself grimly.

Peta found herself the centre of attraction. The news of Noel Frensham's sudden lightning courtship and marriage abroad spread like wildfire through his circle of friends and acquaintances. 'The bride' was called upon. And Peta, to her dismay and embarrassment, was forced constantly to accept warm congratulations and to play in earnest her unwelcome part of the doctor's 'newly-made wife.'

She wondered how many times she had shaken hands and said: 'Thank you very much,' when some doctor friend or doctor's wife wished her happiness, or how many more times she would hear what a 'marvellous man' Dr. Frensham was, and what a lucky girl *she* was. She grew bored by the continual sounding of Noel's praises, and the assurance from all sides that she had married one of the finest men in the world.

No doubt it was true. Indeed, she began to wonder why this marvellous person should be in the least concerned about her, and why he did not let her go quickly and quietly. She supposed she should be flattered, but all she wanted to do was to get away.

The news spread, of course, to her own particular friends, who inquired for news of her from the Bradleys and were sent on to Dr. Frensham's house. Some girl with whom she had been at school . . . some woman who had been a friend of her mother's or father's . . . some man who had known her in the old days . . . each and all came along or wrote to her and showered her with hearty congratulations. They expected her to be happy. And in order to prevent discussion or scandal, for the moment, she endeavoured to play the role properly, to smile, to appear as contented as the world assumed her to be.

It was all a strain, and there were times when she felt like dashing out of the house to some place where she could be alone. Yet where could she go? Only to the aunt in Devonshire, and that meant she would be a long way from Auburn. Besides which she had no job, no money. Every day she felt that she was sinking deeper into the quicksand of this marriage until there were moments when she feared that it would close over her head and swallow her up completely, and that she would never make her escape.

Noel, except for that look of strain, behaved with remarkable calm, and seemed to find no difficulty in pursuing his own role of the happy husband.

Whenever the occasion demanded he was ready with a charming word about 'my little wife,' quick to put an arm about Peta's shoulder, ignoring her confusion. He seemed to wish to maintain the illusion that he had 'married for love.'

When they were alone, he gave no sign whatsoever of the feeling for Peta which had been revealed to her on his first night home. He was friendly and courteous, but no more. And he made it hard for her to fight him. He avoided any discussion about Auburn or their future. The only time that they had a real argument was on the subject of money. Peta was being proud and refusing to accept monetary gifts and he grew angry about it. She must, he said, buy herself clothes which befitted her position. She *was* his wife for the moment, whatever she would be in the future, and she need feel no compunction about taking it, he said.

When Peta stubbornly rejected the offer, he threatened to go to shops and send her home a dozen dresses on approval, and then through sheer feminine vanity and the fear that he would choose something that she hated, she was forced to give in to him.

That very next day she appeared in a new, charming summer outfit, cornflour blue with touches of black—a small black hat and a short blue coat to match. The ensemble was beautifully cut, and made her look a little older, a little less the simple child and more the chic woman about town. She entered Noel's presence somewhat reluctantly, her face expressing both embarrassment and mutiny. But Noel took no notice of that and was warm in his praises.

'How lovely you look,' he said. 'I'm glad you were so sensible, and I admire your choice. I shall be proud to introduce you to Edith this afternoon.'

With a sense of shock she remembered that his sister was coming to tea that afternoon. She drew off long black suède gloves, took a cigarette from the box on Noel's desk and lit it with an irritable gesture.

'I honestly don't see what's to be gained by all these meetings and introductions.'

'I've rather enjoyed them,' said. Noel. 'I had no idea how "social" I could become. It's a pleasant change having a wife about the house, instead of rushing off to hospitals and nursing homes.'

'Oh dear,' said Peta with an exasperated sigh. 'You *are* a peculiar man.'

He laughed at her, stretching his legs before

211

him, hands in his pockets.

'And you are *very* pretty, Peta. It would seem much more comprehensible to the world if I had to divorce you for running away from me than if you divorced me for leaving you. Why should a tired, middle-aged physician leave a girl who looks as charming as you do?'

She coloured to the roots of her hair.

'You flatter me!'

'When's Lyell expected back?' he asked abruptly.

'The end of this week.'

'Better have a serious talk with him and find out definitely what he means to do about things.'

There was nothing Peta wanted more. But she wondered, wretchedly, if perhaps Auburn might find it very awkward to be mixed up in a divorce suit. Was business as bad as Noel thought? Would it affect Auburn's attitude? But no, she told herself fiercely, he would, he *must* take her away. She couldn't go on like this. It wasn't fair to her, to Noel, to any of them.

In her bag was a letter which had come from Auburn this morning. He had kept his word and written her lavish, passionate love-letters. But even those had not altogether comforted her. She noticed that *he had signed none of them.* That had seemed to her odd. There were neither dates nor addresses in any one of them. Just odd slips of paper scribbled with extravagant expressions of love and longing.

Was it for a moment possible that Auburn did not want to get himself involved with her—did not wish to be compromised by signing his love-letters? Oh heavens! She mustn't allow herself even to think such a thing—or to suspect that any of the disparaging remarks Noel had made about him were true.

She felt immensely depressed, this afternoon. The strain of the past few days, the whole uneasy position was getting her down. And quite suddenly she dropped her bag and her gloves and, covering her face with her hands, burst into tears.

Those tears had a devastating effect upon Noel. He had never been able to bear seeing a woman cry. To see this one, whom he loved, break down so unexpectedly, to see that pretty figure in the charming new dress shaken with sobs, tore his very heart strings.

He got up, crossed to her, and put an arm about her shoulders.

'Peta, my *dear* child, what is it? What's the matter?'

She kept her face fast hidden, but he could see the big tears trickle through her slim fingers. She sobbed brokenly:

'I'm so unhappy . . . it's all so . . . so wrong and hateful. Oh why, *why* did I ever marry you?'

Frensham's tired, clever eyes darkened with pain. How it hurt him to hear her say that! He

213

kept his arm about her.

'Do you hate me so much, Peta?'

'I don't hate you at all. You're frightfully kind and I know you're good, but oh . . . it would be so much easier if you didn't hate Auburn so violently.'

He stiffened and drew away from her.

'Afraid I can't help that, Peta. I have reasons for hating him, and they can't be disposed of, even to make you happy.'

She lifted a face childishly disfigured with weeping. Taking her hat from her head, she shook back her curls.

'I can't go on like this. Something must be settled.'

'Then settle it with Lyell when he comes back.'

She dried her eyes vigorously.

'I will. He must take me away—quickly.'

Noel picked up the half cigarette which Peta had placed in an ashtray when she broke down, and took a breath of it.

'And just supposing that Mr. Auburn finds it inconvenient to be cited as a co-respondent. What then?'

'Then you must let me divorce you. You must! You must!' she said in a broken, excited voice.

'I see. And blacken my own character, which is very important to me as a medical man, just for the purpose of seeing you led down the garden path by a man who has no

214

intention of marrying you?'

'But he *will* marry me!' she cried wildly.

'All right, Peta. On the day he takes you to his home and introduces you to his people and tells them that he means to marry you as soon as you have divorced me . . . I'll do it.'

She caught her breath and pressed her hands together.

Hope revived in her. She had got her way— as Auburn had wanted her to get it. She had made him see that it wasn't fair to make things so difficult for her. She was positive, when Auburn heard, that he would take her to his home, and announce that he meant to marry her as soon as she was free.

She felt a good deal happier all of a sudden. She must see Auburn and tell him of her victory the moment he came home. And she felt suddenly warm and grateful towards Frensham. Impulsively she held out her hand.

'Noel, that's marvellous of you. I do appreciate it. Honestly I do.'

He thought:

'She doesn't care about me at all. And supposing the fellow *does* agree? Then I shall lose her for ever. Yet somehow I don't think he will. And I'm still gambling on that.'

And Noel felt that that gamble was still very much on later the same afternoon when his sister came to tea.

Edith was eight years older than Noel. She was a cold, hard woman with a superior manner and a touch of snobbishness which was foreign to Noel's nature and which annoyed him. Owing to the difference in their ages, he had always, even as a small boy, stood in awe of Edith, and curiously enough he still felt a trifle uneasy in her presence. There had never been any great affection between them. They were temperamentally poles apart, and she had been jealous of his mother's adoration for him from the time of his birth.

Since he had made a big success as a doctor, however, she had thawed considerably towards Noel, and when he made a will in favour of her son Kenneth, she was nicer than he had ever known her. He knew that the news of his marriage had shocked and disappointed her, because she had looked upon him as an incorrigible bachelor, and of course she would realise according to the terms of their father's original will, Peta, as his wife, must automatically inherit everything.

That alone would be sufficient cause to estrange Edith from him, and he did not suppose that this afternoon's visit would be a pleasant one. Well, he was quite prepared to face that, although he did not wish her to upset Peta, and he knew she was only coming out of curiosity to see 'the bride.'

The tea party could not be called a success. Peta, although elated by what she considered her recent victory, felt nervous and self-conscious at this introduction into a family which she meant to leave almost immediately. It gave her a guilty complex. She felt vaguely that she was making such a fool of Noel, although it was his fault and not hers, she argued with herself. And she found Mrs. Powell unapproachable, icily polite and obviously resentful of her. It had, however, the effect of making her feel sympathetic with Noel. It was pretty rotten for him that this woman should be his only living relation. No wonder he was a lonely man. And, of course, when Peta went away with Auburn, Noel would be lonelier than ever. She was quite surprised to find what a friendly and compassionate spirit his sister's visit awakened in her. She made herself particularly nice to Noel during the tea which they had in her boudoir, and nobody was more surprised than Noel when Peta addressed him so genially, and occasionally he caught a kindly glance from her big brown eyes—those expressive eyes which were so much too lovely and attractive to him.

'Isn't it marvellous that Noel made such a recovery in Port Said?' she said on one occasion.

And Edith's stiffly polite reply was lost upon him because he was thinking:

'Anybody'd believe she was really glad I lived, but I don't think she can be!'

Mrs. Powell stirred her tea and turned the conversation to what she called her brother's 'amazing leap into matrimony.'

'You can imagine how astonished we were,' she said. 'Why, you only knew each other for a few days on board, didn't you?'

'Yes,' said Peta, and came to an abrupt end of her chatter.

Noel said:

'I fell in love at first sight, Edith.'

'Well, you didn't waste time,' she said with a slightly malicious smile.

'No,' said Noel. 'It doesn't do to miss your best opportunities, and I wasn't going to let Peta out of my sight.'

Two pink spots appeared in Peta's cheeks. Mrs. Powell retained her smile and recalled something that her son had said last night about this girl catching Noel when he was too weak and ill to realise what a fool thing he was doing. She had to admit that Noel's wife was very pretty and quite a 'lady.' They wouldn't be ashamed of her in the family, although it didn't seem to her that she was at all the right sort of wife for a distinguished physician. She was too young and lacking in the 'grand manner.'

'What are your plans for the immediate future?' she asked, making an effort to be agreeable, because Kenneth had asked her to.

'You don't want to quarrel with Uncle,' he had said before she left. 'He might hand out the odd tenner at Christmas and on my birthday, even if I'm not his heir any longer.'

Noel looked at Peta.

'We aren't quite sure of our plans,' he said slowly. 'Although what I'd like to do is to get away up to Scotland, and have some fishing and see what sort of prospects there are for the grouse season.'

Mrs. Powell turned to Peta.

'You'll find Glengelly Lodge a fascinating place,' she said. 'My son Kenneth has had many happy days there with his uncle.'

'And I hope will have many more,' said Peta politely.

'I look forward to showing Glengelly to Peta,' said Noel. 'I bet she'll fall for my pack of Cairns and particularly for my Jonnie.'

Peta murmured something. She had heard so much about Noel's favourite dog that she felt that she knew him. But it was all so unreal and stupid, this farce of pretending to be Noel's wife in earnest. And it was really distressing to her to realise that Noel was absolutely sincere in his wish to take her up to his place in Scotland and introduce her to his dogs. He was such an essentially nice person. Oh, what a mess it all was!

And it was still worse when Edith Powell leant back in her chair, looked up at the mirror with the two candlesticks and said:

'Dear me, I never look at that without thinking of poor mother's sentimentality about your birthday. Do you remember how she insisted on lighting the candles even when you were a grown man?'

'Yes,' said Noel, 'I'm not likely to forget it.'

'Are you carrying on the tradition?' Mrs. Powell turned to Peta.

Peta said impulsively:

'I think it was rather a beautiful one.'

'And what is more,' put in Noel, 'she did carry on the tradition very charmingly, and lit them for my birthday the other day.'

Peta thought:

'Burn would curl up at this sort of conversation.'

She tried to make herself go all hard and feel that it was all rather sentimental and stupid, but she couldn't. It appealed too much to all that was soft and romantic within her.

She was thankful when Mrs. Powell took her departure.

'Your sister hates the sight of me,' she told Noel frankly.

'She has no cause to,' he said. 'At least, not from a personal point of view.'

'She'll certainly have no cause to when she hears that our marriage is coming to an end,' said Peta. 'That'll put her boy back where she wants him to be.'

He looked at the pretty flushed face and felt a very real throb of pain.

'God!' he broke out before he could restrain himself. 'I wonder if you realise how little I want to do that and how much I want to keep you with me.'

Something induced her to go up to him and

220

put a hand on his arm.

'I'm awfully sorry, Noel. Things have worked out rottenly for you, but it never entered my head that you—'

'That I'd want to turn this marriage into something more than a farce? No, I don't suppose it did enter your head. And you'd better not worry about it now!'

He spoke with a savageness that startled her, but almost immediately apologised.

'Sorry! It isn't your fault any more than mine. We both thought I was passing out, and here I am very much alive, and you're in love with Auburn Lyell and that's that! Thanks for entertaining my sister and not giving the show away. I'd like her to suppose we had some kind of happiness before the bust up of our marriage. Will you excuse me, my dear . . . I've got some letters to write.'

He was out of the room before Peta could answer. She stood a moment staring after him, her brows knit, her heart jerking uneasily. It made things so embarrassing and difficult to realise that Noel minded as much as this, that there must be an end to their marriage. And whatever she felt about Auburn, however madly she was in love, she could still find it within her to like and admire Noel and to hate the thought that she, in some way, was responsible for that look in his eyes, that almost tortured look which had been there just before he rushed away from her just now.

Simultaneously she was filled with a longing for Auburn and that assurance of love which every woman needs from her lover . . . needs again and again and yet again! She found her eyes filling with tears, and through those tears came a blurred vision of the candlesticks in the gilt mirror. And she had a sudden childish, sentimental wish that Noel's mother could come alive, and stand here and talk to her for a moment, and help her to put things right.

She found herself whispering:

'I don't want to hurt him. I didn't mean to. It's just happened this way. And I don't want to hurt myself. I love Burn so much.'

And the next minute she was curled up in an arm-chair with her face hidden in her hands, crying as though her heart would break.

CHAPTER FIFTEEN

The duration of Auburn Lyell's business in Manchester lengthened from a week into two weeks. As the days went by, Peta grew more and more unhappy and uneasy. She still heard from her lover, but the notes were pencilled— just two or three words of passion or flattery which left her curiously unsatisfied. Added to which, her position in Noel Frensham's house became more difficult with every day that passed. She kept meeting more people, more of Noel's friends and acquaintances. And the longer that she remained here, the more she seemed to consolidate the whole business. Indeed, so used was she becoming to her name, Mrs. Frensham, and the role which she filled as the doctor's wife, that she felt in some fantastic fashion it was all becoming a fact.

Since that one outburst from Noel on the day of his sister's introduction to her, he had made no effort to remind her that he wanted her to stay, or that he resented her desire to go. He was friendly and nice—but with reserves. She was frankly miserable and anxious for Auburn's return.

She had meant to wait until she saw him to tell him that Noel had changed his mind and that the divorce could be on her side, providing that he received proof that Auburn meant to marry her. But she sat down and wrote her lover a long letter of many pages, telling him everything that had been said between herself and Noel.

'Write by return of post and tell me how soon you think we can fix things now, because I can't go on like this, darling,' she ended that letter.

To her surprise and distress Auburn ignored both the news and the request. The reply which she received to her letter was no answer at all. It merely told her that he was 'crazy to hold her in his arms again.'

For the first time since she had fallen in love with Auburn, the shadow of a doubt crossed her mind. A doubt as to whether he did really love her as she loved him. But so appalling was that shadow that she drove it away and refused to let it return. Burn was just waiting until he saw her. Men didn't like to say things in letters. Yet *why not*, if this one was serious and looked upon her as his future wife?

Her wish to see Auburn lost some of its rapture and became almost a pain. But she would have died rather than let Noel see what she felt or even guess that that horrible doubt had for the fraction of an instant shaken her faith in Auburn.

How long would his business detain him? How long before she could have everything out and he could ease her mind and her heart with the proof of his love?

At the end of the second week there seemed no sign of Auburn's return to town.

Then Frensham began to notice things. To notice, for instance, that Peta was losing her appetite, losing her lovely colour, and that there were bluish shadows under her eyes as though she had been sleeping badly. A new look of strain in her eyes. He had said nothing all these days, but he had watched. He was well aware that she heard from Auburn and equally aware that she was fretting because of his long-continued absence. It would be no astonishment to Noel if Lyell let her down . . . just as he had let down the others. But any exultation that he might have felt when it struck him that he was having a pretty safe bet with life and himself, faded at the sight of Peta's distress. She was trying so bravely to conceal it from him. Poor child! He wished to God that he could help her. He had been pretty positive from the beginning that her love for Lyell would lead her into a hell from which he, Noel, could not save her. His tenderness for her increased every day that she spent in the house with him, and it was no small hell for him to have to sit and watch her gradual disillusionment.

Of course he might be making a mistake. Perhaps Lyell was involved in business difficulties from which he could not extricate himself easily. He knew that the firm was rocking. But that seemed no reason why he should let a single doubt creep into Peta's mind.

There came a morning when, over the breakfast table, Noel mentioned Lyell.

'When do you expect him back?'

Peta, who had been sitting very still and with a taut look about her mouth, flushed and avoided his eyes.

'I'm not sure.'

'Is he still in Manchester?'

'No, he's gone on to Birmingham.'

Noel drank his coffee. He felt horribly sorry

for her. Oh, damn this fellow Lyell! Why had he this atrocious power to hurt defenceless women? If only he could be Peta's defence. He loved her so much that he really, honestly believed he would give her up gladly if he could be sure of her ultimate happiness.

'You'll be wanting to get things fixed with Lyell fairly soon, won't you?' was his next remark.

'Yes,' said Peta.

'If I were you I should suggest that he takes a train down to town and sees you for an hour, even if he has to go back.'

'Yes,' said Peta in the same stiff little voice, 'that's a good idea. I will.'

She went out that morning to the nearest post office feeling almost desperate. She knew perfectly well that Noel suspected Auburn of playing fast and loose with her affections, and all her woman's pride rose in revolt. It wasn't true. She was going to prove to Noel that he was wrong. She was hot with resentment as she walked down Wimpole Street, thinking out the telegram that she would send to the last address which Burn had sent from Birmingham. She must tell him that it was imperative that he should return and talk things over with her; that she could not go on like this. Or perhaps she could get him on the telephone. A personal call. She knew that he was at the Queen's Hotel. She also knew that on his own admission he was not a man who rose early.

226

She would probably catch him in at this hour, ten o'clock. She could of course go back to the house and put through a call from there, but Noel would probably be busy. The phone would be in use. Besides, she wanted a very private and confidential talk with Burn this morning.

So worried and miserable was Peta that she did not notice the beauty of the summer morning. A lovely London morning. The sky, of pearly transluscence, was shot with blue, with that faint haze heralding heat. Sunlight flashed on the chromium of the long low cars purring up and down the busy street in the heart of the medical world.

For all Peta knew, she might have been walking through the rain. The beauty of life and living was eclipsed by the anguish in her mind. Her feelings towards Auburn had reached a pitch of sheer agony. She didn't want to doubt him. She kept telling herself that she did not doubt him. And yet he seemed to have deserted her, and all his passionate promises had thinned down to the mere artificial expressions of a love which wore the cheap flagrant colours of insincerity.

If Burn was indeed not as wholly and genuinely in love with her as she was with him, it would be intolerable, not only because she cared for him with all the intensity of her nature, but because he would be letting her down where Noel was concerned. She would have to admit to Noel that he was right, after all her furious denunciations of his allegations against her lover . . . after all her defence of Burn.

'He can't let me down,' she whispered to herself as she turned into Wigmore Street. 'He mustn't . . . oh, but he won't!'

In the post office she put through the personal call to Mr. Auburn Lyell.

'Shall we pass your name?' she was asked.

And when she said 'No,' that added to her mental disturbance because it was almost an admission that if Burn thought the call was from her, he might refuse to take it.

While she waited in the crowded post office for the call to come through, she walked up and down telling herself that she was being ridiculous. Burn was just busy and couldn't get back to see her. She was allowing herself to be influenced by Noel's quiet persistence that Auburn wasn't worth while.

Peta paced up and down, no more conscious of her own beauty than she had been of the glory of that tranquil summer's day. Yet not a man who entered the post office but cast a second glance at the slender girl in the grey flannel suit with the little sports felt at a jaunty angle on her dark curly head, struck perhaps by something unusual in the pale young face with the brown serious eyes and the red, perfect mouth—lips curved for pleasure—and for pain. There was a hurt look about her

228

today—a tragic air which seemed incongruous with all her lissom youth and loveliness. And that drew the gaze of women as well as of men, and made them wonder who she was and what lay behind the mute protest of shadowed eyes and hurt red mouth.

Then suddenly her heart gave a wild leap. A man leaned across the counter and said to her:

'Your personal call to Mr. Auburn Lyell. No. 1 box, please.'

Peta came alive. Flushed, starry-eyed, flinging off the tragedy, enveloping herself in sudden wild excitement, she shut herself in the stuffy little box, which was almost unbearably hot, and picked up the receiver with a trembling hand.

Two red lips were close to the transmitter now . . . as close as they might wish to be to the lips of her lover who was at the other end of the wire, hundreds of miles away.

'Hullo,' she said. 'Hullo . . . Burn . . .'

Then Auburn's familiar voice, astonished:

'Good Lord, Peta, is that *you*?'

'Yes,' she said breathlessly. 'Oh, Burn, can you hear me?'

'Sure. This is a surprise! How are you, my sweet? Where are you?'

'In a telephone box in a post office near home.'

'Anything wrong?'

She might have said a dozen things at once and yet her heart was rejoicing and her whole body burning, because he had called her 'sweet' and she did not think it possible now that he had changed. But she had to be sensible and come down to brass tacks and she knew it. So she blurted out:

'I must see you, Burn.'

'Why?'

'You haven't answered my last letter.'

'Yes I have.'

'Darling, no,' she said, her throat constricting. 'I mean about *us*. We've got to settle something. I can't go on like this, living with Noel.'

'*Living*...'

'Oh, you know what I mean!' she protested. 'I can't go on pretending to be his wife. It isn't fair on either of us. Besides, he has offered to give me a divorce straight away, if you will tell your people and announce our engagement. I told you that in my letter and you didn't answer.'

Now there was silence at the other end of the wire. The palms of Peta's hands were wet. Her whole body was drenched with perspiration in the heat of that little box and from the intensity of her feelings.

'Are you there?' she asked wildly. 'Burn, did you hear me?'

He answered. His voice seemed to her colder, more distant.

'Sure I heard and I am here.'

'You must come,' she said in the same wild

230

voice, 'and I must know what you mean to do. You do love me, don't you?'

'Yes.'

It wasn't a very convincing affirmation, she thought. It was all horribly unsatisfactory, this shouting at each other in a long-distance call. She had asked for six minutes, reckless of the extravagance. She would have another six if necessary, but she must make Auburn see that they couldn't go on with the situation as it was.

'Burn,' she said, 'you've simply got to come down to see me, if only for an hour or two.'

'Listen, angel,' came Auburn's protesting voice. 'I'm horribly busy . . . stuck up in the Midlands . . . I can't possibly get away, and I don't see what use it is, my coming down for a couple of hours. Anyhow, we've talked it all over before and decided that we'd wait.'

'But, darling . . . that was because you didn't want the divorce to be the other way round, and your reputation to suffer. But it's different now. I tell you Noel will give us the divorce, but he insists on you taking me to your people first.'

Again a silence. Peta felt near to fainting in the intolerable atmosphere of that box. Or was it because her emotions were almost killing her? It was so cheapening, so degrading to be howling down the telephone like this for an assurance of her lover's sincerity. She couldn't bear it.

The conversation went on. Auburn didn't

want to come to London. Auburn said he was too busy. Auburn advised her to lie low and wait a bit, wait anyhow until he did see her.

*   *   *

The six minutes were up and frantically Peta asked for a further call. The longer she spoke to Auburn the less loverlike he seemed, the more irritated by her demands. He was not as she imagined he would be, surprised and enchanted by her news about the divorce. He didn't seem to want to take her to his people. He didn't seem to want *her* so much. And then when she gasped out an anguished appeal for his love and support, he became more like the old Auburn and told her that he adored her and always would, and that if she insisted he would come down and see her. But if she'd wait, he expected to get his Birmingham deal through by the end of the week, and then he'd be back. He wasn't going to the old home. His family got on his nerves, he said. A pal who was abroad had lent him his service-flat in Lion Court, off Curzon Street. He would be there by Saturday at the latest and would give her a ring, and then they'd straighten things out.

'Am I to tell Noel that you'll do as he asks?' Peta demanded, feeling that she had got nothing out of this call.

Auburn's reply was haughty.

'I won't do what anyone asks. I'll do what I think best.'

That left her speechless. Then Auburn made one of his highly artificial speeches about 'giving a fortune to hold her in his arms again and aching to kiss her' and a lot of things that for some dark dreary reason brought no comfort to Peta's bursting heart.

'Good-bye, little sweet,' he ended, 'and we'll fix up something so that we can be together.'

And that was all that he said and the 'something' might mean anything, but he gave her no reason to suppose that he intended to take her on Noel's terms—only his own.

She was frightened, frightened and ice-cold when she hung up the receiver and paid for that call. There was nothing left of warmth or radiance, nothing even of the tragic anticipation which had given her an air of glamour when she had entered the post office. She was a white, cold, expressionless girl, moving out into the increasing warmth of the sunny morning, retracing her footsteps to Wimpole Street.

She didn't know what to think, and tried not to think at all. She only knew that Auburn had evaded straight questioning and seemed to be playing for time, and she could not understand and dared not try, neither did she know what she was going to say to Noel when he questioned her.

She could only presume that she had

233

worked herself up into this feverish suspicious state, and that there was nothing at all behind Auburn's attitude and conduct except the faint irritability of an extremely occupied business man who could not, in the middle of important business, be worried with his personal affairs. It didn't seem very fair on her, but she supposed she ought to try to be sympathetic with his side of the show, and he *had* said that he still adored her and that they must soon be together.

This was only Monday. She wouldn't be able to see him till the end of the week. And then he would be coming down to a flat of his own, and perhaps when they met he would see that something must be done and give Noel sufficient proof of his integrity towards her, so as to induce him to give her her freedom at last.

But the Peta who walked automatically with a set, drawn face back to Frensham's house, found it quite impossible to get up any real enthusiasm or belief in herself or Burn or anything. She felt frozen and afraid . . . a hundred times worse than she had felt before she put that call through to Birmingham. For during that call, and she knew there was no use blinding herself to the fact, Burn had somehow or other failed her.

*   *   *

Up in Birmingham, Auburn Lyell returned from the telephone box to the dining-room and resumed the large breakfast on which he had just been about to start, when that personal call came through.

He took his seat at a small table opposite a girl. A girl with hair of metallic fairness parted in the centre and twisted into a silken knob at the nape of a very white neck. Her features were perfect with the exception of her mouth, which was large, greedy and over-red, and her lashes were too black and sticky to be genuine. Nevertheless she was smartly dressed and striking enough to be the centre of attraction in that room. She raised a cup of coffee to her lips and smiled at the big fair man whose blue eyes looked at her a trifle sulkily.

'Say! You look as though your news wasn't too good,' she said in a high American voice as metallic as her hair. 'Lost a dear relation, honey?'

'Gained a packet of trouble,' he grunted.

'One of your women?' she giggled. 'You have so many, Burny, you're bound to get yourself into a jam sooner or later.'

'Huh,' he said and attacked his eggs and bacon viciously. 'Talking of jam, I prefer sweetness to interference from you, my little one.'

'And you get it,' she said. 'And more than is good for you. What other girl would leave a nice cool apartment in town, and in this heat wave, to follow you round the Midland hotels?'

'Angel,' he said, and broke into a smile. 'You've been grand and I adore you.'

He really felt at that moment that he did. The last couple of weeks had been pleasantly intriguing. The fair-haired girl with the baby face and the sticky lashes was not only an attractive companion, but she was Cathleen Markstein, an American Jewess, daughter of Markstein, the canned fruit king of Chicago, and worth a million dollars. It was the dollars that made Auburn forget that 'Kitten,' as he called her, had a few wrinkles round her eyes, wasn't much under thirty, and was as notorious for her affairs as he for his. She was crazy about him. She wanted to marry him. And he was seriously considering it.

Of course she hadn't any of Peta's attractions. With very real regret he compared the little Jewess with that other girl who had all the freshness, innocence and fragrance of apple-blossom unfolding in the spring sunshine. He waxed quite eloquent about Peta in his mind. But, by heaven, he wasn't going to be drawn into divorce and marriage with a woman who hadn't a penny. He hadn't a penny himself, and he wasn't meant for love in a cottage—not he. A pity! He'd see Peta when he got back and make a tremendous effort to induce her to run over to Paris with him on that job which was waiting for him when he

236

was finished up here. Kitten wouldn't know. And he was loath to say good-bye to Peta for ever before he had shown that heaven of love he'd promised her. For her sake as well as his. He became quite a philanthropist in his own mind. It would be damned unkind of him to leave her to that stuffy doctor—and she did respond so deliciously to love-making. No, he wouldn't part with her before he had made an effort to overcome her scruples without landing himself in for that divorce.

'Say, Big Boy,' Miss Markstein's voice cut in on his reflections, 'who do you love?'

Auburn's heavy lids drooped. His handsome face creased into a smile that made him look sardonic. He raised his cup of coffee to her.

'Kitten!'

'On the keys?'

'On the level,' he said slickly.

Then they both laughed. But in London a girl named Peta began to wonder if she would ever laugh again.

CHAPTER SIXTEEN

When Peta got back to the house she shut herself in her bedroom and refused to appear for lunch. She sent a message down to Noel to say that she had a headache and was going to lie down.

He respected her wishes to be undisturbed until after tea, and then when she still remained in her room he gathered that something was wrong, and that the 'something' was connected with Auburn Lyell.

He went up to her room. He found her door locked. That annoyed him. Why should she lock her door? He had respected her wishes ever since he returned from Port Said, and had never given any cause to believe that he would intrude upon her. And it hadn't been an easy fight—that battle with himself and his increasing passionate love for her.

He was growing tired of the battle and weary of the whole situation. Peta could not go on like this. He knew that most of it was Lyell's fault, but Peta must make her decisions one way or the other. Noel knew that he couldn't stand living in the same house with her under these conditions much longer. He was wholly in love, and neither his return to work nor his renewed health could absorb him to the exclusion of all thoughts and longings for Peta. He knocked on her door.

'Will you let me in, Peta? I am sorry you are not feeling well. I want to talk to you.'

'Is it important?' came from Peta in a small voice.

'I know that something has happened, Peta,' he said quietly. 'You are not really ill.'

Silence. Then:

'I am better by myself.'

'I don't agree. Let me in, there's a sensible child.'

Another silence. A pause. Then the key was turned in the lock. Noel walked into the room. His wife's bedroom! How queer that seemed. This was the first time he had been in it since it had been his mother's room. Very altered now, modernised with cream-washed walls, rose and cream curtains of heavy silk, and the lovely Queen Anne furniture that Mrs. Frensham had collected.

An essentially feminine room full of Peta's personality, he thought, as he glanced round and had a confused glimpse of perfume bottles, cream jars, powder bowls, a dozen and one little oddments of vanity on her dressing-table; some dainty silken clothes flung across the bed, and Peta herself, standing in a queer attitude of defiance and misery, facing him. Her curls were dishevelled, her face bore traces of violent weeping. One hand clutched a dressing-gown of apple-green velvet closely about her white slenderness.

He had seen her before in that very same dressing-gown on board ship, when, in the guise of ministering angel, she had come to his cabin to see him through some of those ghastly nights of fever and pain and delirium.

The remembered vision brought a sharp pang to his heart, but the sight of her misery, all for another man, played havoc with him. He said:

'Look here, Peta, what's happened? You went out directly after breakfast. You're upset. Is it Lyell?'

Peta, having cried until she was sick and blind—cried more with fear than with certain knowledge of her lover's disloyalty—nodded her head dumbly.

Noel drew near her.

'Have you seen him?'

'No.'

'You have spoken to him?'

'Yes, on the telephone.'

'Why did you go out to do that? Were you afraid I'd listen in?'

She flushed dully, and her lashes flickered.

'No. Oh, let me alone, please.'

'I'm sorry, my dear, but this concerns me as vitally as it does you. I want to know how I stand. I want to know how we both stand. I can't go on, and obviously neither can you.'

She started shaking.

'I've nothing definite to tell you. Nothing.'

'Is he willing to take you on my terms. Has he agreed to acknowledge you to his people?'

'I—I—it was so difficult to arrange things on the phone. He is coming back to town on Saturday. I'll see him then.'

Frensham's pulses quickened. He felt that it was as though her words opened gates to him and showed him victory beyond. He had defeated Lyell. He knew it. Peta knew it too, but she was too proud and too desperate to admit it.

Perhaps it was his own thwarted desire for her which made Frensham want suddenly to be brutal. He said, brutally:

'Lyell's letting you down, isn't he? You know it.'

She put the back of her hand against her lips. She yearned to deny it and to fight him. She wanted to hate him. To protest against his brutality. But she seemed incapable of doing anything but look at him with her large wounded eyes. Something in those eyes broke Frensham's resistance. The next moment he gathered her into his arms and was holding the slim velvet-clad body close against him.

'Oh, my poor darling. Poor darling child. I love you so much! I'd give a fortune to spare you from this, but I have seen it coming. He *is* letting you down. You know it. You know it won't be any use your seeing him on Saturday. Peta, darling, I'd do something for you if I could. I can't bear you to be so damnably unhappy.'

She made no effort to release herself from his embrace. She was so tired and unhappy, lost and bewildered by her doubts and fears and the feeling that her big romance was shattering to a thousand pieces before her very sight. With all sex feeling obliterated, she clung to Noel as she would have done to a brother. She knew that he was good and kind and reliable and that he loved her. She needed the comfort of his arms. She put her face against his shoulder and sobbed. Between the sobs she tried to gasp out denials that Auburn had let her down. It was just her nerves getting the better of her, she said. Things were sure to come right. But even while she was sobbing those words she was aware that they were futile, and that Noel knew it.

It was a moment of mixed bitterness and triumph for him, to hold her in his arms and feel her sudden dependence upon him. But he cursed Lyell under his breath as he stroked her curly head and tried to calm her down.

She seemed unconscious of the fact that his lips strayed to her hair, and were pressed for an instant in almost anguished feeling against the smooth ivory of her forehead. He wanted so much to kiss her mouth. But she drew away from him and flung herself on the bed.

'Oh, go away, go away and leave me alone!' she said frantically.

'Listen, Peta. Be sensible. Surely you're not going to let Lyell crow over you. You know it's the end. You can see it coming, can't you? Whatever was said between you over that telephone has shown you that it is coming. Do you want to crawl to him and let him kick you away because he is tired of you?'

Peta sat up, eyes blazing through her tears.

'You shan't say such things! I don't know it's the end. *I don't!*'

Frensham felt pitiless again.

'Yes, you do. And you're my wife. I won't have my wife brought to her knees by that scoundrel. Let the end come from you. Don't wait for Saturday. I implore you not to wait.'

Peta felt driven beyond endurance.

'I must see him. I must. You shan't stop me!'

He took her by the wrists and pulled her back into his arms, and now there was a fierce quality in the gesture with which he caught her close to him.

'I haven't stopped anything, so far. I haven't felt that I had the right to, because you made a mistake in marrying me, but I would have given you everything through my death, and I want to give you everything now that I am alive. But you're selfish and heartless except where that rotten cheap trickster is concerned. And I can't stand any more of it. I know what he is. You refuse to see, even though it's been brought under your very nose. I tell you, Peta, I won't have my wife crawling to him. You're mine, *mine*, do you hear me?'

Aghast, she made no effort to release herself. And for a reckless moment Noel let himself go. He rained kisses on her pale tear-wet face and on her soft throat. He knew that he must have hurt her by the fierceness of his caresses. And then, when a little protesting cry came from her, his blood cooled and he let her go, not knowing whether he hated or loved her, confident only that he hated himself for his loss of control.

243

Spent and sick at heart, he faced her, panting.

'I am sorry,' he said. 'I suppose I ought to remember that you're not my wife in any more than name, and that I shouldn't care what the devil you do. Go to Lyell. Go, for God's sake, and let there be an end to it.'

With these words he flung out of the room and the door closed behind him. Peta sat on the edge of the bed with her face in her hands. It was a long time before she could stop trembling. She was horrified at the way everything was turning out. It didn't seem to her possible that there could be so much dreadful emotion, such a conflict of human sensations in the world. And Noel's outbreak of violence left her both astonished and dismayed. She could not be angry about it. She knew too much now about the pain, the agony of unfulfilled love. These last few days of her life had taught her how one could suffer over love and what despair could do to one, and how the mere idea of losing the beloved could eat like an acid into one's very soul. Love, as she had wanted it, was a beautiful thing of passion combined with friendship, and of infinite tenderness. It was a creative and joyous thing. But these feelings that she had now for Auburn, *this* kind of love was wholly destructive. And Noel was being destroyed too. They all were.

She wouldn't wait till Saturday. She would

put another trunk call through to Burn. She would tell him that she was ready and willing to leave Noel's house at once and go to him, if he still loved her.

It was six o'clock. After seven, Burn would probably be back in the hotel, having finished his day's business.

Peta pulled herself together, walked into her bathroom and lay for some minutes in a hot bath full of verbena salts, her swollen eyes shut. Her limbs ached as though with fever, but she knew that this fever was of the mind, not of the body. And while she made her wild little plans to run away from Noel and go to her lover, she thought, too, of Noel. She thought:

'Poor Noel! I wish I could have loved him. I wish everything could be different. That nobody need be hurt. But life's like that. It must always hurt someone. There must always be the odd man out!'

Her plans were mad, of course. She contemplated going up to Birmingham on the night train. She must see Auburn and be reassured; she could barely live through another night of doubt and suspense. Noel might say that she had no pride. Perhaps she hadn't. At least not that sort of pride. She just loved. A woman must forfeit her whole heart when she loved—and pride must go to the wall, too.

By seven o'clock she was dressed in a suit

ready for a journey, even with a hat on her head. White and tense she put that call through to Birmingham, and this time risked finding him in and did not make a personal call.

Now it happened that at the precise moment when that call reached the Queen's Hotel, Auburn Lyell was in his bedroom dressing to take Cathleen Markstein out to a show. He was getting into a dinner jacket. He was tying his black tie whilst his 'Kitten,' already dressed and looking marvellous in a skin-tight dress of 'off-white' satin, and an ermine cape around her bare shoulders, sat on the edge of his bed watching him tie the bow, and telling him what a big, big, handsome boy he looked. She liked him in his shirt-sleeves, she said, and he had the look of a naughty little boy about him.

When the telephone bell shrilled out, Auburn said:

'That'll be about our seats. I asked them to phone me if they could get anything nearer the front row. Answer it, angel face.'

So it happened that Peta's call was answered by a high-pitched American woman's voice, and not by Auburn's as she had expected. For the telephone operator had said that he thought Mr. Lyell was in his bedroom and he would switch her through.

Cathleen said:

'Hullo.'

Peta said:

'Oh—I—I must be on the wrong line.'

Cathleen Markstein's pretty painted face tightened. She said in a dangerously sweet voice:

'Were you wanting Mr. Lyell?'

'Yes. Is he there?'

'Sure he's here. And who wants him?'

'It doesn't matter about the name. Just put me through please.'

'Oh, is *that* so,' drawled Miss Markstein.

Auburn Lyell shot round from the mirror.

'Who is it, Kitten?'

'A very charming girl,' Cathleen answered, but her rouged lips were not smiling.

Auburn's ears tingled.

'Who the devil . . .?' he muttered, then stopped.

An imp induced Miss Markstein to say down the telephone: 'Mr. Lyell wants to know who the devil it is.'

'Shut up, idiot,' said Auburn, and made a grasp for the receiver.

Cathleen said:

'Not so fast. Are you double-crossing me? Have you got some girl in London wanting a private talk, because I'm not standing for that. If you're going to marry me you'll cut out all the other dames you've been fooling with.'

All of which conversation was plainly overheard by Peta at the other end of the wire; Peta sitting on her bed in the big London house

247

that lovely summer's evening, with the sun still shining, and a deathly cold feeling in her heart. She sat like one frozen, staring before her. So there was a woman in Burn's bedroom—an American girl who said he was going to marry her. That certainly was interesting! Then Peta began to laugh hysterically. She just managed to put the receiver down and cut off the call, then pressed both clenched fists to her lips to keep herself from screaming as the wave of hysteria drenched her.

She lay face downwards on the bed and stuffed a pillow against her mouth to deaden the noise of her own crazy weeping. All the time her mind was a tangle of thoughts. A confusion of sensations storming her. She kept sobbing to herself:

'So Noel is right. He is right. Burn is all that he said. A cheap trickster. And this ends it all ... oh, Burn, *Burn.*'

While she lay there, crying, the telephone bell rang. She pulled herself together sufficiently to answer it. The housekeeper's voice said:

'A personal call from Birmingham for you, madam. Shall I switch it through?'

Peta sat bolt upright and drew a hand across her smudged, tear-stained face. She felt as though the fount of her tears had dried up. She felt nothing but coldness and lassitude. This was Auburn. Well—she would hear what he had to say. But it would not make any difference. But she was without emotion now. Like a dead thing. She told Mrs. McLeod to switch the call through.

Auburn, having escaped from Cathleen Markstein for five minutes, had put that call through from the bar where no women were allowed. He was in a cold sweat. He knew that Kitten had 'mucked things up,' damn her, and he didn't want to lose Peta in quite that way.

He said, excitedly:

'Peta . . . hullo, Peta . . . is that you, my sweet?'

Peta set her teeth and said:

'It is Peta, yes. What do you want?'

'Look here, I want to explain. This is all a mistake . . . a joke . . .'

'Rather a poor joke,' Peta cut in. 'And I don't think I'm making a mistake. There was a girl in your room and she said you were going to marry her. That's enough for me.'

'I tell you it was all a joke . . .'

'I don't believe you. And I don't ever want to see you again.'

'So that's what your love's worth, is it?'

Peta laughed—a terrible little laugh.

'Yours was worth so much that you couldn't come down to face a crisis with me. No— because you had another girl with you in your hotel.'

'Oh, hell . . .' began Auburn furiously.

'That,' said Peta, 'as a place, would be too good for you. Good-bye, Burn. You needn't worry about me any more. But it would have saved a lot of trouble if you'd been straight with me from the beginning.'

'So that's your line, is it? Maybe you've discovered you want to link up permanently with that smug doctor you've married.'

'He isn't so smug,' said Peta. 'But he knew all about you, and I thought he was lying.'

'So he was! Damn it, I—'

'Good-bye,' said Peta in her strange, cold little voice and hung up the receiver.

The bell did not ring again. The bedroom was very silent. The shadows of the summer day lengthened and the light changed from dark gold to a shadowy blue. The whole house seemed very quiet. Like an automaton, Peta began to take off her travelling suit and change into a dinner frock. She did not know which dress she took from the wardrobe. She did not care. She could hardly manage, because her fingers trembled so.

She knew that she must go downstairs and face Noel—Noel who hadn't lied and had warned her, all the time, to expect this. She didn't want to face him. She felt too utterly dejected—humbled to the dust because the man she had loved and trusted had justified every one of the unpleasant truths that Noel had said of him.

As she turned to the door, forcing herself to take action, there came a knock and a maid entered with a letter on a salver. Peta took it without interest. Then she saw that it was not a stamped letter, but a note, and in Noel Frensham's handwriting. She looked up quickly at the maid and said:

'Is the doctor downstairs?'

'No, madam. He went away a few minutes ago and asked me to give you this note.'

Peta swallowed hard. She did not care to question the servant so she dismissed her. But she felt her cheeks growing hot as she ripped open the envelope. She could imagine what had happened. After the last scene with her, Noel had decided to go away. She had driven him out of his own house.

She read the letter, written in his small, decisive handwriting.

'Peta,

'I can't stand any more of this and I don't suppose you want to share a house with me under these circumstances much more than I do with you. I have cancelled all my engagements and am going up to Glengelly Lodge where I can be quiet and alone.

'You seem sure of Lyell, so I take it for granted that you will fix things up with him and that he will look after you. I would like to wish you happiness, but I can't. I don't think I'm a very unselfish type of fellow and I definitely resent handing you over to a man like Lyell. But I'd like you to remember that I love you and, unfortunately, I always will.

251

I don't reproach you. The initial fault was mine in asking you to marry me, therefore I must accept my defeat.

'You shall have your divorce. If you give me breathing space, I'll send you the necessary evidence.

'N. F.'

Peta looked up from that letter and stared across her shadowed room. Her breath came quickly. Her eyes were luminous in the dark. Although her body and soul had seemed stunned by the pain of her own defeat, she was still able to appreciate the fact that somebody else was suffering; that Noel's defeat must to him be as bitter as her own. He was a proud man and a lonely one, and she was the first woman he had loved and wanted for his wife.

'*I don't think I'm a very unselfish type of fellow,*' he had said in his letter. But that wasn't true. He was utterly selfless. He loved her and he was willing to give her a divorce—ready to sink his pride and sully his reputation as a doctor, by going through all that sordid business of 'faking the evidence.' It was unspeakable—an outrage, and she was sunk with shame at the mere idea that she had ever wanted him to do such a thing. How could she have been so mad as to suppose that she could be happy with Auburn, having ruined such a man as Noel Frensham? How could she ever have been at peace with her own conscience?

In this bitter hour of stark realisation, of knowledge about Auburn, herself, Noel, so many things that had been hidden from her before, Peta came to a deeper understanding of life itself. She began to see that passion—the tempestuous emotion she had felt for Auburn, that almost slavish emotion—had been mere infatuation and not love. Love was a finer thing. It was love that Noel Frensham had given her, because he was willing to obliterate himself for her. With that knowledge, there also came into Peta's young, ever-romantic heart, a burning desire to show Noel that she was grateful to him. Somehow she must make up to him for this. Somehow she must make him understand that she was ashamed of herself for ever entertaining the idea of such a sordid unfair divorce, and that he must not go through with it now, no matter what happened to *her*.

All her life Peta had been impulsive. It was a terrific impulse now that led her to ring the bell frantically for Mrs. McLeod, and while she waited, tore off her chiffon dinner dress and got back into that tweed suit again. She was still dressing when Mrs. McLeod entered the room. Peta said:

'Mrs. McLeod . . . you know the doctor is going up to Scotland tonight. What train is he catching . . . what station does he go from? Please help me, because I must see him before he starts. It's very important.'

Mrs. McLeod regarded her young mistress a trifle coldly. There was a good deal of gossip going on in the servants' hall about a 'tiff' having taken place between the doctor and his wife, and it was generally supposed that the doctor had gone off in a 'huff.' Mrs. McLeod did not approve of any woman who upset her precious doctor.

She knew all about that train. It was the night-express which the doctor often caught when he went up to his lodge for a long week-end. She gave Peta the information and then offered to pack for her. Peta shook her head ...

'I'm not going to Scotland. I only want to see the doctor before he goes.'

Mrs. McLeod raised her brows at that, and left the room in a cold but respectful silence.

CHAPTER SEVENTEEN

Noel Frensham stood smoking a cigarette on the platform, just outside his carriage in which the porter had placed his suit-case and golf-clubs.

He looked gloomily at the crowds around him. There is nothing much more depressing, he thought, than a dark, noisy station platform, even on a fine June evening. And he felt ill and tired. Ill with mental strain rather more than any organic trouble. He was really fitter, physically, than he had been for some time since his return from Port Said. But he felt rottenly depressed and nervy. He was smoking too much. When he had finished his cigarette, he flung it away with an angry gesture and told himself that he must 'let up.' He was a fool to allow the thought of Peta to upset him like this. She wasn't worth it. She was going to Auburn Lyell, and he, Noel Frensham, was a sickening ass to behave like a lovesick boy. The sooner the divorce was over the better.

He had felt that he must get away from that house in Wimpole Street and from the strain of having to see Peta all day, and know that she was sleeping under his roof. Never had he needed the quietness and peace of his beloved Scottish moors more than now. Yet never had he looked forward to going up there with less enthusiasm. God! what a miserable thing it was for a man to be in love with a woman who was his wife, and to whom he meant less than any of these people passing up and down the platform . . . strangers whom he would never know.

Then he saw Peta . . . Peta in her tweed suit, and fox-furs, hurrying down the platform towards him. In astonishment he watched her approach. She had seen him now. He greeted her, his heart thumping badly at the mere sight of her.

'What on earth is it, Peta? What's brought

you here?' he asked.

She looked up at him with a flushed face. Now that she was beside him she was a mass of embarrassment and knew not what to say. She stumbled out a few words:

'I got your note . . . I had to come . . . There's something I want to tell you.'

'What is it, Peta?'

'Just this. I . . . you mustn't send me that evidence. I . . . that is . . . if you want things to stay as they are . . . so do I.'

He looked more astonished than ever.

'What do you mean? Don't you want the divorce?'

She shook her head.

'No. No. Not any more.'

He caught her hand.

'You don't mean that you want . . .' Then he stopped, gave a dry laugh and flung her hand away. 'No, of course not. This isn't because you want to stay with me. Something's happened between you and Lyell, eh?'

Her head drooped and her face went scarlet.

'Yes. We're through. I found out that all you've said about him is true. I don't suppose there's time to tell you the details before the train goes. I just found out by a mere fluke, that's all.'

'I see,' said Frensham.

He stood up, cold and straight. This was the victory which he had planned and which he had wanted. Queer how flat it all fell and what little satisfaction he got out of it. But because he loved her, he felt a pang of pity at the sight of her humiliation. He said gently:

'Well, you know I can't be surprised about that. For your sake, I must say it's as well it has all happened now before you burned your boats.'

She did not meet his gaze. She played nervously with her fur.

'Yes. It would have been awful if it had happened later.'

'It would have ruined you, Peta. He wrecks every woman he touches.'

Then she looked up at him.

'I'm not glad because of that. I've been a crazy little fool and I deserve to be wrecked. But I'm glad because of you. It wouldn't have been fair for you to go through with that divorce. I see that now.'

Her eyes told him that she was being sincere, but he shrugged his shoulders.

'I would have given it to you.'

'I know that. I came to thank you but to ask you not to do it. Oh, I expect you're sick of me—you'll want to be alone. I can always go away. But if I stay as your wife—we could save any scandal . . . for you . . .'

He looked at her curiously . . .

'Are you really thinking of me?'

'Yes,' she said wretchedly. 'Try to believe me. I must have seemed frightfully selfish. But

I'm not as bad as you think.'

He felt all his latent tenderness for her sweep into his heart. He ached to take that forlorn little figure in his arms and kiss away that hurt, blind look of misery which was stamped upon her face.

'Oh, my dear,' he said, 'I don't think you're bad at all. You were just infatuated with the fellow. I'm sorry if you're miserable about it, but don't you think, really, that you've had a lucky escape?'

'I suppose so,' she whispered, and hung her head like a child, ashamed.

'Listen,' said Noel, 'I don't want a divorce. And as I told you long ago, I'd like things to stay as they are. I'm not going to ask you to fall into my arms, but if we stay together we could be friends, couldn't we?'

Peta felt a surge of misery and of pleasure combined as she heard those words. The tears rushed to her eyes.

'I've always thought of you as a friend.'

'Then that's a bargain . . .'

He broke off. The guard was whistling and waving his flag.

'The train's going,' said Peta. 'I'd better say good-bye.'

Noel's heart began to thump again.

'But why? Why sit at home alone and mope? Why not come with me? It'll do us both good to have a change of air, and perhaps we'll learn to know each other a bit, walking over

258

those moors with the dogs. Come on, Peta, jump in. I'll soon get another sleeper for you. Hurry up.'

Her heart was thumping, too. She gasped:

'But I've no luggage.'

'We'll wire Mackie to send it up on the next train. Will you come?'

Helplessly Peta allowed him to take her hand. He pulled her into the corridor of the train. It moved out of the station slowly. She had to cling on to his arm, she was trembling so. And she did not see a thing because the tears were blinding her.

*   *   *

Two weeks later.

A man and a girl with three wheaten-coloured Cairn terriers racing in front of them, came walking over the moors down a hill towards a stone-built house which faced one of the loveliest lochs up in the Highlands.

The sun was setting and the western sky was streaked gorgeously with red and orange light. The glow of it suffused the moor. The green was flecked with purple. The still waters of the loch were turning slowly to gleaming pearl and silvery pink.

From the tall chimneys of the house a faint spiral of lilac smoke curled invitingly up to the sky and suggested a peat fire which would be welcome, for in spite of the warmth of the day, it grew cold here after sundown.

Peta looked with a rapt expression at the scene before her. Hands in the pockets of her tweed coat, she walked lightly and happily beside Noel, who carried a gun and a bag containing a couple of rabbits.

'What a place this is!' she said. 'I don't think I shall ever get used to admiring it. It's so beautiful.'

Frensham stopped and she paused with him. Together they looked down the winding footpath of the purple moor on to the grey roof of Glengelly Lodge, and beyond to the shining loch.

'You say that after two weeks,' he remarked. 'I say it after two years. I bought this place two years ago. And I expect I'll be saying it after twenty-two if I'm still alive. It *is* the most beautiful place in the world.'

'We've had such a lovely walk—spoilt only by the death of those two poor bunnies!'

'I rather agree with you. The older I grow, the less I like shooting. I think I'll take to fishing.'

'That's just as cruel.'

'No, fish are cold-blooded. Rabbits are warm little things. But don't let's go on talking like this or I shall give this brace a decent burial and refuse to hand them over to cook for a pie.'

Peta laughed. Their eyes met and they both smiled at each other. It seemed to Noel that he had heard Peta laugh quite often during this past fortnight, and that quite often their gaze met in a spirit of comradeship.

He had never enjoyed a fortnight more. He had stamped down the emotional side, and been content to look upon Peta as a friend; to accept her companionship in the spirit in which it was given.

He had never seen her look so well. Her cheeks had filled out. Her face wore a delightful tan and she seemed already a part of Glengelly and this Scotland, which was an integral part of him.

Had she forgotten Lyell? No, that was too much to hope for in so short a time. But she never spoke of him, and if she grieved she did not seem to shed a tear. She had been carefree, like a child, walking with him, following the guns when he went out with a shooting party, or sitting beside him when he fished in his trout stream, or learning to take the oars in his boat on the lake.

Tomorrow he must go back to London and to work. He felt infinite regret at the thought. He put the pipe which he had half taken from his pocket back again. He said:

'Have you really enjoyed being up here, Peta?'

'Every minute of it,' she said without hesitation.

She meant it. She felt almost as though she had been living in another world. She had come up to the Highlands feeling bruised and battered, drained of every emotion except regret. A regret as deep as it was bitter that she had wasted so much love upon Auburn Lyell. And something approaching fear as well. Yes, she was afraid of herself because she had made such a mistake. She could no longer trust her own judgment in a man. That was an awful feeling.

On the other hand, as soon as she had reached Glengelly, the regret and the fear seemed to pass from her. Something in the peace of the moor, the tranquillity of the loch and the brave heart of Scotland had taken away the bruised sensation and given her back her peace of mind.

Then there was Noel . . . Noel, who had proved himself during this fortnight a grand companion as well as a man in whom a woman could place infinite trust. He had been a friend such as Auburn could never be. He had shown her the things he loved and taught her to love them too. This was the sort of life she had always wanted to lead—not that artificial, highly-coloured existence which Auburn would have led. This was her *milieu* . . . this Scotland . . . this was the real Peta, striding over the moors through sunshine and rain, going back to peat fires, sitting there reading or sewing while Noel smoked his pipe.

One of the Cairns came bounding up to her, barking joyously. Noel's favourite terrier, with

262

black, upstanding little ears and bright, dark eyes.

She bent to caress him and he licked her hand.

'Darling Jonnie!'

Noel's heart warmed to that.

'You and Jonnie are grand friends, and you're the first person he's ever deserted me for. I'm quite jealous.'

'You needn't be,' Peta said with a smile. 'If it really came to it, he'd follow you to the ends of the earth.'

'He'd be a silly little dog.'

'He'd be sensible,' said Peta. The words slipped out before she realised she was saying them.

Noel gave her a quick look.

'Why do you say that?'

She flushed.

'Maybe I think it.'

'Why, Peta . . .' he began, and paused awkwardly.

She felt awkward, too. Yet something deep down inside her made her say more.

'Noel, I do want to thank you for this fortnight and for all you've done for me.'

'I've done nothing.'

'Much more than you'll ever know. You've shown me realities. You've shown me how one ought to live, and you've made me realise what silly, cheap ideas I used to have about life.'

'No, you hadn't. You've always had very nice

ideas.'

'They went very wrong, Noel.'

'We all make mistakes,' he said.

'Please believe,' she said, 'that when we get back to town I'll do everything I can to be-whatever you want me to be.'

Frensham drew nearer her. He felt himself beginning to shake. The tranquillity of the moors and the spiritual quality of loveliness in that rare summer evening in the Highlands ceased to exist for him. He was aware only of Peta, standing there close to him, her dark curls uncovered and her small tanned face full of earnestness raised to his. The old wild longing for her came pell-mell upon him. He knew that friendship was not enough and that he wanted Peta for wife, as well as comrade.

'My dear,' he said, 'this fortnight has meant a terrific lot to me and you're not the only one who has learnt things. You've taught me quite a lot, too. I want to make you happy . . . as happy in London as you've been up here.'

'But I am—quite happy, and will be in town,' she said.

He took both her hands and pressed them.

'If I could only believe that there was a chance for me . . . a chance to make you *entirely* happy, Peta. I know I'm a fool. It's much too soon . . . but if you'll just give me hope . . . that's all I want, my dear, all I want!'

Peta looked up at him. For a moment she saw not Noel's thin brown face and grave, kind eyes, but the fair, handsome, arrogant one of the lover whom she had once loved so wildly. It was as though Auburn came and stood there, in Noel's place, a cruel ghost, mocking at her. Yet the mockery did not hurt and the ghost had no power to disturb her. That passion was dead . . . dead and for ever gone. That was what happened to passions of that kind, she thought. They could die as swiftly as they were born. But real love could never die. In this instant, Auburn's ghost faded and left her for ever, and she knew that one day very soon she would learn to love Noel with a love that would last until death—and then Beyond.

Quite simply she put her arms around his neck.

'I don't deserve that you should want me,' she said, 'but if you do, my dear, please take me and never let me go.'

'Peta!' he said under his breath.

Then she was folded in his arms and his lips were upon her curls and he became alive again, not only to the rapture of holding her and to the infinite promise in her words, but to the loveliness of the sunset hour. Here in Glengelly he had always found pleasure and relief from the strain of his life as a medical man. It seemed natural that here, too, he should find ultimate happiness. What more could a man want than the promise of arms and lips from the woman he loved?

'Peta!' he said again. 'My wife!'

265

For the first time she kissed him of her own free will, and was content in his embrace.

The three terriers lay down, put their heads on their paws, and watched the two figures that had merged into one, wondering when it would be time to start the walk again. From the hills behind them came the tinkle of sheep bells, and a little wind sprang up suddenly, bringing with it the fragrance of heather.

We hope you have enjoyed this Large Print book. Other Chivers Press or Thorndike Press Large Print books are available at your library or directly from the publishers.

For more information about current and forthcoming titles, please call or write, without obligation, to:

Chivers Press Limited
Windsor Bridge Road
Bath BA2 3AX
England
Tel. (01225) 335336

OR

Thorndike Press
295 Kennedy Memorial Drive
Waterville
Maine 04901
USA

All our Large Print titles are designed for easy reading, and all our books are made to last.